Other than Honorable

by

Matt Hardman

© 2024, Matt Hardman

All rights reserved. No part of this publication may be reproduced or distributed in any form or by any means without written permission, except in the case of brief quotation embodied in critical articles and reviews that include credit to the author and source.

The content within this publication may not be regenerated, repurposed, or processed using AI in any capacity, as this work is not part of the public domain. To avoid doubt, this work may not be used in any manner to train AI technologies to generate text, including, without limitation, technologies capable of generating works in the same style or genre as the work.

Library and Archives Canada Cataloguing in Publication
Hardman, Matt, author
Other than Honorable / Matt Hardman

Issued in print and electronic formats.
ISBN: 978-1-998501-34-2 (paperback)
ISBN: 978-1-998501-35-9 (ebook)

Cover Design: Paul Hewitt
Interior Design: Richa Bargotra

Double Dagger Books Ltd.
Toronto, Ontario, Canada
www.doubledagger.ca

Table of Contents

Prologue | Soochow Creek

Captain Everett "Ridge" Frost, United States Marine Corps, shouldered up under one of the large front windows of the warehouse and checked his watch, cursing. His team was behind schedule. Nearly an hour behind. The path to this point had been long and stressful, but uneventful. Unwilling to send his men straight up the bridge where most of the Japanese fire was concentrated, he'd led his twelve-man team in a long, winding loop along the Shanghai waterfront, using a thick stone balustrade as cover. Several blocks west of the bridge, they'd made their way down a short dock, slipping into the foul water of Soochow Creek and using a series of abandoned boats, skiffs, and barges as cover to make their way to the far bank. They'd emerged soaking wet and stinking and, most importantly, unseen and had used back alleys and a warren of small shops and restaurants to make their way here, to their primary objective.

"No idea how many inside, sir?" It was Sergeant Randolph—Frost's younger half-brother—tucked in close against the near wall.

Frost shook his head. "Nope." He thought for a moment. "Randy, do me a favor?"

"Sir?"

"Keep that big head of yours down in there." Frost smiled. "Mom'll kill both of us if something happens to you."

Randolph shook his head. "Nah. You were always the favorite."

Sure, I was, Frost thought sourly. He turned back to the window. Checked his watch again. Went over the plan in his head one last time. Not much to it, he thought. Not much more than a military version of a snatch and grab. A robbery. Three squads. Three access points. Collect the principals—a Chinese banker named Liu Qian and his family—and kill anything wearing the wrong uniform. After that? Haul ass back to the bridge, where a spotter would call in artillery to cover their crossing.

One more check of the watch. Thirty seconds.

———

Thirty-year-old Liu Qian sat, huddled and shaking, in the darkened corner of what had been some sort of warehouse. He was filthy, bruised, and battered. He was bleeding. The external wounds—a split lip, some abrasions on the left side of his face, an eye swollen shut, and a gash on the back of his scalp that was trickling blood down his neck and collar— were painful, but nothing serious. The internal wounds were the problem. He had, he suspected, more than a few broken ribs. His breathing was strained and painful and difficult. But again, he told himself, not life threatening. Broken ribs could be endured. They hurt, but they would heal. The real problem, as far as Liu was concerned, was whatever was going on in his abdomen. There was a fire there that common sense told him could not be good. Like he'd sucked down a gallon of gasoline on some epic bender and then chased the drink with a box full of matches. Something, somewhere in his guts, was injured badly. Bleeding, he suspected. And probably profusely. The result of more than an hour of abuse at the hands of his captors.

He lifted his chin to look at them. Saw the man in charge. Not Japanese. British. Called himself Gerald.

What in the hell was an Englishman doing working for the…

The force of the explosion behind Liu caused his handlers to drop him and triggered a wrenching pain in his guts. He was thrown forward by the blast, colliding with the blur that had to be Gerald and knocking him to the ground. A second explosion followed, then a third, both further away.

The gunfire started, crackling shots from every point of the compass. Liu could hear the wet slap of bullets impacting flesh and he cringed, curled on the floor. Beside him, he could feel Gerald—that's who it had to be, he thought—moving, crawling. To his other side, screaming, he could just make out his daughter's tiny form, still kneeling. He reached, ignoring the searing pain in his torso, and yanked her roughly to the ground.

Frost popped up in the broken window as soon as the first explosion ripped through the opposite door of the warehouse. He scanned, his Thompson up and snugged in at his shoulder. There were ten uniformed bodies on the floor closer to the far door. Elsewhere, he saw men racing this way and that, searching for cover as the second and third satchel charges exploded. His men were entering the room now, weapons high and barking as they searched for targets and cover. Another ten Japanese went down in the barrage of gunfire the Marines were laying down. More scrambled for cover and…

There.

Closer to the side wall, the one without a door. Four individuals in civilian clothes.

"Let's move," Frost barked to Randolph and Gonzalez as he rose and entered through the window. His feet hit the ground and he moved left to cover, firing at a group of three Japanese troops huddled behind a crate. He hit two of them and watched as the third pitched forward, shot by Randolph.

Frost crouched behind a crate, peeked, checked on the civilians, saw that they were still huddled on the floor and not moving. Good. He continued left, dashing from cover to cover in a zig-zagging path, firing at anything that popped up.

To his front, a Japanese soldier appeared suddenly, racing around the same stack of crates Frost was heading for. They collided at speed, crashing to the floor. Frost lost his helmet and his grip on the Thompson in the collision and landed on top of the soldier as gunfire raked the crates to his right, sending splinters flying into the side of his face. He ducked closer to the man on the floor, grappling with him. The man recovered quickly. His hands came up, grabbing for a hold on Frost. Frost lashed out with a vicious right hook, heard the crack of the impact against the man's jaw. The soldier caught hold of Frost's collar and tried to throw his own punch. Frost deflected the blow by tucking his right shoulder in and down.

The man twisted, threw a second fist. Frost trapped the man's arm under his right armpit and lashed out with a left jab. The man's head bounced back against the concrete floor and his left hand lost its grip on Frost's collar. Frost threw two more hard jabs square into the man's nose, felt the body tense and then go limp. He leaned close, grabbed the man's head in both hands, and twisted the neck violently.

Randolph and Gonzalez came sliding around the edge of the crate as Frost rolled off the dead soldier. Randolph kicked the Thompson within Frost's reach and glanced at the dead man.

"Hell, Ridge. Lots easier if you shoot 'em."

"Smartass." Frost checked his weapon and worked to regain his bearings. He edged around the crate, saw that Sergeant Miller's team was up and moving, sweeping further in from the warehouse's rear door. Sergeant Barnes's team was covering the building's east exit. And the civilians were still there, just about five yards away, nearly motionless on the floor.

"Only a couple left, sir," Gonzalez shouted. Frost turned his head. What opposition was left—maybe five or six individuals—had been neatly herded into a corner and were pinned down.

Randolph yelled to make himself heard over the racket. "Maybe we should collect those civies and get the hell out?"

Frost nodded. "Good idea. Let's move."

They stayed in a crouch, moving the last few steps behind cover as much as possible, standing only when Miller yelled.

"Clear!"

The phrase was echoed several times before Frost directed his men to the south door of the warehouse.

Frost approached the civilians with Randolph and Gonzalez. One of the civilians was clearly dead. She was face down in a spreading pool of blood and the back of her head was a wreck. The other three were moving. Two men, a woman, and a small child.

"Randolph. Gonzo. Get them ready to move. We leave in sixty seconds."

Gonzalez moved to assist the first man and the child. Randolph moved over to where the third live civilian was pulling himself upright.

"Christ, sir," Randolph yelled. "This fella here is white."

Frost looked over to where Randolph stood, saw the man stagger to his feet. He locked eyes with the man, saw what he took for panic there. The man backed away, slowly at first. Then faster. Moving toward the door.

Well, Frost thought, he'd just sat through the middle of a gunfight. Probably rattled. Frost looked harder at the man. No, he thought. That's not it. Something else there.

"Sir?" Frost started moving toward him.

The man bolted, racing for the door and disappearing into the daylight beyond.

"Jesus, sir," Randolph said, watching. "What the hell do you suppose his problem is?"

"No idea." Frost turned and walked to Gonzalez. "Let's get these folks ready to move, Gonzo."

Gonzalez looked up. "The girl's no problem, sir. She might be forty pounds, at most. But this guy." He gestured to the man. "Someone did a number on him. He ain't walkin' nowhere, sir. We gonna have to carry his ass."

Frost thought for a moment, looked up. "Barnes!"

The sergeant trotted over, took a look at the scene. "Christ, sir. This our target? He don't look mobile."

"We're gonna have to carry him out, Sarge. Pick a couple of guys to trade off. Block at a time."

"I can do that." Barnes looked over his shoulder. "Don't suppose we're going the shortest way back to the bridge now, either."

"Back the way we came, Sarge. Minus the swim if we can avoid it. Let's get moving."

———

Brigadier General Albert Whitehead had moved forward, was now in the same room Captain Frost and his team had occupied two hours earlier.

"Where in the hell are they?" he growled at no one in particular. He checked his watch. "More than an hour late."

The roar and volume of gunfire had increased steadily over the previous fifteen minutes. Japanese artillery shells were slamming into the building with greater frequency. The air was thick and humid and reeked of smoke and cordite and whatever was rotting away in the river to the building's front. Dust hung heavily in thick, swirling clouds. Chips of concrete, brick, and plaster flew, pinging off of walls and nicking bits of exposed skin.

"Sir! I think I've got 'em!" one of the lookouts screamed.

Whitehead moved in a crouch, nearing the lookout. "Where, son?"

Both men ducked as a fresh cascade of gunfire scoured the building's crumbling façade.

"Bit west, sir. Headin' for the bridge, sir," the corporal wheezed. "Just not comin' down the main road."

Whitehead lifted his head, cautiously, trying to get line of sight on his men. It took three tries, but he finally saw them, crouched and moving, maybe thirty yards west of the bridge abutment. Whitehead patted the corporal on the shoulder and began moving back to the charts and the radio he'd had wired to this temporary post. He was halfway there when he heard a sound that made his blood run cold.

He turned, started to raise his binoculars. He stopped when one of the lookouts screamed.

"Armor inbound!"

"Almost there, sir," Corporal Miller said.

Frost glanced ahead, saw that the mouth of the bridge was maybe ten yards off. He nodded, patted Miller on the shoulder, kept moving forward, checking behind him every other step to make certain that he had everyone. He reached the corner of the abutment and paused, letting his team stack up behind him. He waved Barnes forward, watched as the man crab-walked his way to the front of the column.

"How are the guests doing?" Frost asked, yelling to be heard as shells whistled by and automatic weapons barked overhead.

"Girl is out cold, sir. She's with Bowman. The guy is another story. Screams bloody murder with every step."

Frost nodded, peered around the corner, and turned back. "Just the bridge left, Sarge. We're late as hell, but…"

"We made it, sir. Just a quick jog across, hope like hell no one sees, and we're home free."

Something like that, Frost thought, hoping it went that smoothly.

The gunfire slowed around them. And another sound emerged.

What in the hell?

"Shit, sir," Barnes yelled. "Armor inbound!"

The high-pitched sounds of whistles kicked up. First one, then twenty…Then yelling.

Frost grabbed Barnes by the collar and began screaming. "Across the bridge! Now! Everybody move!"

"Sir, you can't! Captain Frost is still on that side of the—" a major was yelling above the din of whistles and racing diesel engines.

Whitehead slammed his hand down on the map, pointing. "Goddamnit! I said fire! Right fucking here! I want that bridge dropped!"

Frost was one-quarter of the way across the bridge when he heard it. The thundering sound was unmistakable. He threw himself on the deck, taking Gonzalez down with him.

"Incoming!"

The sound was wrong, his mind screamed as he bounced off the road's hard surface. It's coming from the wrong place…

The first rounds landed in a deafening roar. Explosions rocked the bridge, sent pressure waves slamming into Frost's body. He launched to his feet, dragging Gonzalez up with him and shoving him forward on wobbling legs.

"Get off the fuckin' bridge!" he screamed, racing forward, crouching to grab and shove others as he went. "Go! Go! Go!"

More rounds landed, the explosions throwing fire and debris and shrapnel in all directions. Frost dove behind an overturned car, felt tugging and stinging along his left leg. More explosions tore the air.

Frost stumbled to his feet, looked forward.

Twenty yards to go.

His mind raged. He saw Marines down. One there, ripped nearly in half. Another with half his head completely gone. And another, right—

Frost shoved Gonzalez to the ground as another salvo landed. Ahead of him, he saw Randolph caught in the open, racing for cover and then…he was gone. A roar. A flash of white-orange flame. The hypersonic sound of fragments whispering by.

Frost hauled himself up, grabbed Gonzalez and another two Marines nearest him, and shoved everyone forward, racing for the end of the bridge as the world came crashing down on them all.

1 | The Man for The Job

"He's perfect for us," said one of the men in the dark, double-breasted suits. "No living relatives. Father died when he was younger. Brother killed in action in China. Mother died just last year. He's unmarried. Unattached. Not even any close friends. None that we could find, anyway. Not even a girl waiting for him back in Indiana." The man closed the folder in front of him and reached for the pack of cigarettes sitting beside it. He extracted one, stuck it between his thin lips, and lit it with a silver-jacketed lighter. "You see any problems with this, Colonel?"

Colonel Isaac McDonald shifted in his seat and gazed at the three men at the other end of the cheap conference table. He watched the leader of the group suck on his cigarette and exhale. Watched him as he sat there, staring. Waiting for a response.

Who the hell are these men, he wondered. And what do I tell them? How do I tell them?

The problem he saw with the whole operation—if that's what this was, his mind cautioned—was obvious. Or should have been. Especially to these men. Men in expensive suits. With expensive haircuts and expensive watches. Men who had just recited the entire life history of a single Marine officer. Everything from the man's grades in primary school to how many matches he'd once won as a high school wrestler.

So, Colonel McDonald thought again. How to tell them? How in the world do you state the obvious without sounding…

What?

Insulting?

Condescending?

McDonald cleared his throat, a short coughing sound ejected through tight lips and clenched teeth.

"Gentlemen," he said, diplomatically, "Captain Frost is unavailable at the moment."

"And why is that?" asked the smoker, a tall, thin man, with short salt-and-pepper hair and long, aquiline features that somehow shouted affluence.

Southern money, McDonald thought. Old, family money. Plantation money? He shook his head clear of the irrelevant thoughts.

"Mr. Jackson, Captain Frost is currently in the brig at Pearl Harbor, serving the remainder of his sentence."

"Which has been extended four times," said the man to Jackson's right. A short man. Short and stocky and powerful looking. With thick features, broad shoulders, full, brown hair, and that strangely neutral patois that just screamed midwestern cornfield. "We know about the sentence. And we know about the circumstances surrounding it. We also know why the sentence has been extended four times by the brig commander. Why is this a problem?"

The question caught McDonald short.

Isn't it obvious? he thought. Captain Frost was in the brig. He would stay there for the foreseeable future. Marines who ended up in the brig were expected to do their time. No two ways about that.

But the way they're looking at you, Isaac. As if they think you have strings to pull.

Why?

"What my colleague, Mr. Stevens, means, Colonel," said Jackson, indicating the shorter man, "is that we know that Captain Frost has already served eighteen months of what should have been a simple, one-year stint in that brig. We know that Captain Frost was sent to the brig after conviction at a court-martial for breaking the nose of his commander, one Brigadier General Albert Whitehead, for an artillery fire, uh, mishap, shall we say, while stationed with the Fourth Marine Division at Shanghai."

McDonald almost flinched at the bare facts of the statement and the cold way in which they'd been related.

Mishap, he thought. Jesus Christ. Wasn't that the understatement of the century?

The man identified as Mr. Stevens was grinning at him, McDonald noted. He turned his attention back to Jackson.

"…and the four extensions on the sentence, imposed by the brig commander for three assaults on the guard force and several charges of insubordination," Jackson finished. He sucked at the cigarette, exhaled slowly. "We are aware of this. We also understand that, at the completion of his sentence, Captain Frost is to be separated from the Marine Corps with an Other Than Honorable discharge."

"Then why would you want anything to do with him?" McDonald asked.

Jackson smiled, sucked at his cigarette again, and crushed it out in a small, tin ashtray. "I am afraid, Colonel, that that is not something we are at liberty to discuss."

McDonald cocked his head to one side. "Gentlemen, I'm not quite sure how I can help you. Short of the processing of his discharge, Captain Frost will stay in that brig. I don't have the pull to short-circuit something like that."

"No, you don't," Jackson agreed. He pulled a second cigarette from the pack, lit it, and snapped the lighter shut. He used it to point to the door on the right side of McDonald's office. "But your commander does."

Oh, dear God, McDonald thought. They want me to ask General Whitehead to let the man who broke his nose go free. Are they mad?

"I know what you're thinking, Colonel," said the unidentified man on Jackson's left. "Right now, you're thinking we're nuts. Am I right?"

"You want me to…"

"Go ahead," said the man.

"To ask General Whitehead to…pardon the man who…"

Jackson shook his head. He smiled, his cigarette tucked neatly to one side of his mouth. "No. We don't want you to ask the general anything. You are going to tell him."

McDonald nearly laughed at that. "You want me to tell the general? To order him?" A grin escaped. "Gentlemen, I don't think you understand how the Marines work. I'm just a lowly colonel. I don't order flag officers around."

McDonald's argument faded when Mr. Jackson stuck his hand inside his suit coat and withdrew a single, folded sheet of paper. He eyed the document warily, as if it might catch fire. Or bite.

"What's that?"

Jackson placed the paper on the table and shoved it toward McDonald. "Marching orders. For your boss."

"From who?" McDonald rose from his seat, moved around the table.

"See for yourself," Stevens said.

McDonald picked up the sheet, unfolded it, began reading.

It is, on this, the Fifteenth day of August, in the year of our lord Nineteen-Hundred and Thirty-Nine, ordered that one Everett Frost, Captain, United States Marine Corps, be released from the United States Brig at Naval Station Pearl Harbor, Hawaii. It is further ordered that Captain Frost be transported to Washington, DC, to be presented to the Director, Federal Trade Committee, in as expeditious a manner as is possible.

Signed,
Franklin Delano Roosevelt
President of the United States of America
Copy to: Mr. Henry R. Jackson, Director, Federal Trade Committee

McDonald looked up from the letter, saw Jackson watching him.

"I know you have questions, Colonel," Jackson said. "I would too. But this is not the time for questions. That comes later. In your case, maybe not at all. I apologize for that, but you've been in the military for some time now. You know the score. This is the time for action. Do you understand?"

"There is a plane," said the still-unidentified man to Jackson's left, "leaving Honolulu for the mainland in four hours, Colonel. We need Captain Frost on that plane. The rest of the itinerary is on this paper."

The man placed a second sheet of paper on the table. McDonald collected it, examined it, refolded it.

"Can you do this?"

McDonald took a deep breath. He glanced at the two sheets of paper in his hands. It had sometimes been easier, he thought, to get shot at. He swallowed hard. He nodded.

———

"Are they mad?" Brigadier General Albert Whitehead growled ten minutes later. "This man…This son of a bitch…"

"I know, sir," said McDonald. "I know."

Whitehead flopped into his high-backed leather chair, brushed at his white hair with one hand and clutched the paper in his other. "I don't like this, Isaac. I don't like this at all." He held the form in his left hand, frowned at it, slapped it with the back of his right. "What could they possibly want with Frost? What in the world would anyone need him for?"

Because, thought McDonald, before Shanghai, Frost was one hell of a Marine. A poster child. Like Chesty. But with Gary Cooper's good looks. Christ, he thought. They'd approached the command once. Some photographer and a public relations man. Wanting to use Frost's likeness.

But you can't say that, Isaac. Not any of it. Not here. And not to this man. And besides, what would a trade committee need with a Marine?

What the hell was the Federal Trade Committee? And why did those three men look less like bankers and more like…

What?

Soldiers? No, he thought. Not that. Not exactly. But close.

"I don't know, sir." It sounded lame, McDonald thought. Sounded like a dodge. "They didn't say."

Whitehead continued scowling at the paper. "Well, man, did you ask?"

"I did, sir."

"And?"

"And they didn't answer, sir. Not officially, anyway."

"What in the blue blazes does that mean?"

"They just said that they needed him on that plane, sir. And gave me the rest of the itinerary."

Whitehead grunted, read the papers again. "What the devil is this Federal Trade Committee? What would Frost know about trade?"

"I don't know, sir. I've never heard of it."

Whitehead set the sheets of paper down on his blotter. He pressed them flat with the palms of each hand. He leaned back in his chair. "I don't like this, Colonel. Not one little bit." He stood, dug his knuckled fists into his lower back and stretched. "And before you say anything about this being personal, it isn't. Has nothing to do with them asking for Frost. I'd feel the same if it was any other Marine."

The hell you would, McDonald thought.

"Of course, sir."

"We aren't supposed to do business this way. The man broke rules and he's supposed to be held accountable." Whitehead sat back down. "Christ, Colonel. That kid has been a thorn in my side for two years. Two whole years!"

"Yes, sir."

Whitehead picked up the papers. "But still… Signed by FDR himself…" Whitehead handed the sheets to McDonald, reluctantly, as if he was doing so against his will. Which, in a way, he was. "Take care of this, Colonel?"

McDonald nodded, accepted the papers. "I'll make all the arrangements, sir."

"Thank you, Isaac." Whitehead said. "Dismissed."

McDonald turned for the door, walked to it, had just put his hand on the knob when Whitehead's voice reached him.

"And Isaac, I want Frost in front of my desk before you take him to see this Jackson fellow. Understood?"

Though his back was to the general, McDonald stopped himself from grimacing. "Understood, sir."

Captain Frost woke up to the sound of a wooden baton bouncing against the steel bars on his cell door. He did not open his eyes. Did not move. Did not respond to the banging noise or the pitched yelling of the guard. His mind was busy elsewhere. Recalling…

The nightmare, he thought. Same as it always was. Soochow Creek. Shanghai. Nineteen thirty-seven. Fourth Marine division. His squad sent across the creek, six blocks into

Japanese-held neighborhoods, under a murderous crossfire, to pull out a banker named Liu and his family. The crossing. The raid on the warehouse. Finding the bodies of the Liu family.

And the one white man, Frost thought. The man who'd torn off into Shanghai after the gunfight. How odd to see a white man, a civilian white man, in Shanghai.

Then, the exfil. Back to the bridge. Across the bridge. They'd nearly made it when the artillery shells had come shrieking through the air, crashing down as his Marines raced to safety.

Without moving, Frost swore.

Not just artillery. Friendly artillery. Ordered by General Whitehead.

Because he'd panicked.

Friendly fire that had killed Baker, White and Thompson. Rodriguez and Barnes. And Randolph.

Jesus.

First Pop. Then Randy. And then, while he'd been rotting away in this cell, his mother.

"On your feet, Marine."

Frost lifted his head, peered through the dim light of his tiny cell, eyeballed the guard. He waved at the man, closed his eyes, dropped his head back to the sweat-stained pillow. Felt the rough cover and the poking of the occasional feather shaft against his neck and skull. A thought flitted through his mind. He cracked an eye open, checked the guard's sleeve, closed the eye again.

A corporal, he thought. A new one. Immaculate, too. Nice, pressed uniform. Clean shaven. Boots polished as prescribed. Blond. Blue-eyed. Poster boy. Fresh from training or school or something. Complete with that slow, southern drawl. The kind of speech that might make someone question the speaker's intellect, but never his toughness. Mississippi, maybe? Alabama?

And they sent him here, with that stupid billy club, to bang on the iron bars and wake me up. Already had breakfast. Too soon for lunch.

So why is this guy here?

The corporal drew his club across the bars again, the clang-clang-clanging obnoxiously loud in the confined cinderblock space. "I said to get on your feet!"

Frost lifted his head and cracked an eye open again, glancing this time at the calendar tacked to the opposite wall. He dropped his head.

Friday.

That's why they'd sent the kid.

The club ran back across the bars again. Harder. Faster. Short barks of boned wood on the thick iron bars.

Eager little bastard, Frost thought. Angry, too. Why? Because he thought that's how he should act? Or maybe he'd had a bad day. Did it matter?

"Listen, Corporal," Frost started.

"No," the kid cut him off. The voice was loud. Agitated. "You listen. I got orders to get you over to the captain's office. Got orders to get you over there right quick, ya hear? So, on your feet, Marine. Go on. Git up."

Frost propped himself up on his elbows. "What's your name, Corporal?"

The club banged on the bars again. "Don't fuckin' matter what my name is, you sorry sack o' shit. Now, go on. Git up. On your feet."

Frost leaned back, folded his hands behind his head and crossed his ankles. The thin mattress gave way beneath him, straining the galvanized steel links of the bedframe, forcing them to rub against each other and squeal.

The captain wants me.

A fight. Has to be.

Friday Night Smokers on the Pearl Harbor waterfront. On the Row, maybe. USS *Nevada* last time, wasn't it? Who was hosting this week? *Arizona*, maybe? Maybe it would be that big damned snipe they have. Six-two. Two-thirty. Jet-black hair. Square jaw. Arms like sewer pipes and legs like tree trunks. Big old bruiser of a guy. Cocky, too. Doesn't even take his cover off to fight. It just sits there, squared off and low on the brows.

Frost yawned.

Would be right funny to be the first to knock that stupid hat off of the bastard's head. Might even be worth going willingly.

Frost smiled.

Can't do that, though, he reminded himself. Can't go willingly. And why? Captain Hendricks, Frost thought. That's why. A short, angry man. Grounded aviator. Brig commander out here on Oahu. Greedy little sonofabitch. Makes money hand-over-fist at those fights. And maybe at other ventures?

Frost wondered at that, trying to remember if he'd ever heard about any other rackets in and around Pearl Harbor. Near his feet, where the cell door was, the banging of the billy club had ceased and the clinking, clanking noise one associated with large rings of keys could be heard between the muted blusters of the corporal.

"Goddamned sonofabitch… Just wait… Show you…"

He's coming in here, Frost thought. Sure as hell. And without back-up. Just him. All what? Five-foot-six of him? A buck twenty. Buck thirty maybe? And all by his lonesome. Just him and that billy club.

Frost stared at the ceiling and grinned.

Bad move, Corporal.

Frost heard the lock click. He heard the hinged door squeal. He closed his eyes and reminded himself to go easy on the kid. Wasn't his fault.

2 | Smokers

Frost sauntered into the office of Captain Edwin Hendricks, United States Navy, with his hands cuffed tightly behind him, four days of scruff on his jaw, and his brig uniform—a tattered set of black-and-white-striped coveralls—disheveled nearly beyond belief. The guard, a fresh young private named Timmons, stopped a full four paces behind Ridge, intent, it seemed, on keeping himself well out of harm's way.

"And halt," the guard squeaked.

Ridge stopped ten paces from the captain's desk. He waited without coming to attention. Or parade rest.

Ten seconds passed. Then ten more. And then thirty.

Without looking up, Hendricks snarled, "You can sound off any time you like."

Frost said nothing.

Another thirty seconds passed before Hendricks looked up from the paperwork in front of him. He eyeballed Frost for a good, long while before shifting his gaze to the guard. His eyes flared.

"Timmons, who the hell let you on guard duty? Where the hell is Corporal Parks?"

The guard's voice shook, uneven and nervous. "Uh, sir. Corp'ral Parks is in sickbay, sir."

"When the hell did that happen?" Hendricks's voice rose in volume and his face flushed. "How did it happen? Nobody told me."

"I don't know, sir. The medics was takin' Corp'ral Parks out when I showed up, sir. Gunny Harford told me to escort the pris'ner, sir."

Hendricks's eyes shifted, landed on Frost. They narrowed. Were somehow accusing. "You did this, didn't you? Just beat the hell out of one of my Marines?" A pause. A correction. "*Another* one of my Marines."

Frost said nothing.

"Speak, goddamnit."

Frost offered a grin. A thin one. One of those grins that could mean anything, depending on the context. Something sure to infuriate the captain.

Hendricks came out of his chair and moved around the desk with surprising speed. He moved to within seven paces of Frost, but no closer. He was angry, yes. But he was not a complete idiot. He jabbed a finger in the younger man's direction.

"Goddamn you, Frost. That's the third one this month. The third Marine guard that you've beaten to a bloody pulp. What in the hell is wrong with you?"

Frost shrugged, spoke, his voice unstrained, calm. Almost reasonable. "He tried to hit me with a club."

Hendricks let his eyes shift from Frost to Private Timmons and back. He stayed quiet for a moment, then turned and went back around his desk. He collected a cigar from a box near his desk lamp, cut it, lit it, and inhaled deeply. He blew the smoke out in a heavy, blue cloud that the ceiling fan began to stir.

"You're a real piece of work, you know that, Frost? A real piece of work." Another drag on the cigar. Another cloud. "You should have been drummed out of the service by now. Why hasn't that happened?"

Frost shrugged. "It's a damned mystery."

"It's a damned mystery, *sir*," Hendricks corrected. He glared at Frost and then began reciting a memorized litany. "Assault on a superior officer. Seven total assaults on my guards. Gross insubordination. And that's just the tip of the iceberg. Just the tip. The Marines won't kick you out. Or haven't yet. God only knows why. All you have to do is do your time and behave and you could leave the brig, but you won't do that either." Hendricks paused again, puffed on his cigar, clearly waiting for Frost to say something. When Frost offered nothing, he went on. "You came here on a twelve-month stint for rearranging your commander's face after you blamed him for a bad artillery mission. That was eighteen months ago."

Frost felt his skin flush. Felt his pulse twitch. Felt the old anger flare. Artillery, he thought. Images flashed through his mind. Shanghai. The 4th Marines. Skirmishes against the Japanese. And friendly fire. Two full salvos dropped on…

Hendricks was still going. "…Added fifteen days for that little scuffle. Plus, thirty more when you broke Sergeant Jackson's arm. And now, what? Maybe sixty more for this thing with Corporal Parks. Depending on how bad off the kid is." Hendricks turned to Timmons. "What do you say, Timmons? How bad did Parks look?"

Timmons stuttered, flinched when Frost turned to look his way. "P-p-pretty damned bad, sir. L-l-looked like he was dead, sir. His billy club was all broke up too, sir."

New, fresher images flashed through Frost's mind. Parks entering the cell. Parks poking him with the club. Parks swinging the club overhand, intent on...

Who the hell knew what the corporal had intended?

And then there was the surprised-as-hell look on the kid's face when Frost had caught the club in mid-swing, wrenched it from his grasp, and…

Frost smiled again.

Hendricks caught the look. "Think this is funny?"

"It is," Frost allowed. "Just a little."

Hendricks offered his own thin smile. He pointed at Frost with the chewed end of the cigar. "You know what, Frost? I'm glad you beat up Parks. Real glad. Know why?"

"Got a pretty good idea."

"Got a pretty good idea, *sir*," Hendricks corrected again. "That's five more days. Plus, all the other bullshit, and I've got you here for six more months. Six… more… months." He punctuated each of the last three words by jabbing the smoking cigar in Frost's direction.

"Six more months of you making money off my fights?"

Hendricks smiled. He dismissed Timmons, much to the young man's approval. When the guard had left and the door to the office was firmly shut, Hendricks grinned widely.

"That's right, Frost. Six more months of prize fights. Six. Lotta cash to be made down there on that waterfront. Lotta cash. Like tonight, for instance. All the pay clerks on those battleships will be spending the whole day forking over wads of cash to officers and enlisted. And I got you set up with that fella from the *Arizona*. The big sonofabitch. Boiler tech. Eight-to-one odds that you can take him. Plus, some twenty-to-one odds that you knock him out. And nearly thirty-to-one if you down him in the third."

Knew it, Frost thought. "And if I don't?"

"If you don't what?"

"What if I don't put him down in the third? Better yet, what if I just go down myself?"

Hendricks almost laughed at that. He pointed the half-smoked cigar at Frost, chewed end first. "Well, hell, son. Go ahead. Take the fall. Don't put that smug, wrench-turning bastard down in the third. Don't put him down at all. Let him hit you. Let him knock your block off. That's your choice. But then I have to make a choice too, see? I have to decide if maybe you using Parks's own club on him is a bit worse than just using your fists and boots. Like maybe I decide that what you did today ain't simple assault. Like maybe it was attempted murder. Like maybe we set up another little court-martial and I keep you here for a good long while. Years instead of months."

Frost nodded. That was pretty much what he'd expected from this interview. "Fine. The snipe goes down in the third. Can I go now?"

Hendricks smiled, jammed the cigar in his mouth and spoke around it. "Sure. Just as long as we have an understanding."

———

It took Colonel McDonald forty minutes to draft the paperwork freeing Captain Frost from the Pearl Harbor brig and another fifteen to write up the message and orders directing Frost to report to the Commander, War Plans in Washington, DC, as soon as travel could allow. He reviewed everything, had

Brigadier General Whitehead sign it all, listened to the man growl and groan about the whole affair, and walked everything down to communications himself. He handed it off to the clerk and gave directions for the dispatch to be sent as quickly as possible.

———

The crush of people on the USS *Arizona*'s forecastle was amazing, Frost thought. Must be a thousand people here to watch the fights. Officers. Enlisted. Most from the crew of this battleship and from her massive sisters. Some not, though. There was at least one group of nurses. A few Marines. And a gaggle of Army Air Corps pilots was standing off to one side of the makeshift ring, stuffed into the crowd waving cigars and fistfuls of cash.

Fighter jocks, Frost decided as he continued scanning. Had to be.

A collection of pit snipes from *Arizona*'s Black Gang, fireroom and engine room types, huddled around the far corner of the ring. They were a filthy bunch. Sooty, rough, and loud as hell.

Near to his own corner stood a collection of cooks and stewards. Predominately black men. Young. With angry looks on their faces. One of them, Frost noticed, was almost as big as the *Arizona*'s snipe and had been shadow-boxing along with the fight. Mirroring every movement. Much in the way the on-deck batter times the opposing pitcher.

Kid moves well.

Frost smiled and looked to the opposing corner. The *Arizona*'s guy was bleeding. From the nose. From his lower lip. From a gash above his left eye. He was breathing hard. Long, lurching breaths. Struggling to catch his wind. His massive body working double-time to bring enough oxygen in.

A hand grabbed Frost's shoulder. He turned.

"Third round, Frost," Hendricks said into his ear. "Third round. Make sure he goes down."

Frost rose from his stool.

So did the snipe.

The referee, one of the *Arizona*'s officers, pointed at both men, raised an eyebrow, got nods, then waved his hand to ringside.

A bell clanged to start round three.

Frost didn't move at first. He stood there, still and steady, with both arms at his sides as the snipe barreled straight in. The man telegraphed a jab and threw it. Frost slipped it easily and moved right. The snipe telegraphed another shot—a hook this time—and threw that, too. Frost dodged left, hands still at his sides, his shoulders loose and relaxed.

Come on, big boy, he thought. Come on. Two more jabs. Then that big right hook.

Frost danced further left, his feet light and quick. The snipe lumbered after. Heavy. Stodgy. What energy the man had possessed before the fight seemed to be going or already gone. Frost dodged. Circled. Bobbed. And found himself facing his own corner. He could see Hendricks. Could see the *Arizona*'s own captain. Could see a messenger with a clipboard and the two captains talking and Hendricks flushing a bright, angry red…

Well, isn't that interesting…

A blow glanced off of Frost's right shoulder, bringing his attention back to the large man trying to knock his block off. He moved left.

Come on, he urged again. Left jab. Left jab. And then…

It came, just as he'd wished. A monster right hook. Big and looping. Powerful enough to kill. There was rage behind the swing. Uncontrolled anger.

But it missed.

Frost flashed left, side-stepping the blow. His hands came up, one guarding his chin, the other a lightning-fast counter punch that caught the snipe square on the point of his jaw.

The man's face crumpled. His knees sagged. And the snipe collapsed in on himself in a bloody, sweating pile of skin and dungarees and leather.

Most of the crowd groaned. Some of the crowd screamed.

But Frost heard none of it.

He was watching Hendricks.

The captain was apoplectic. He was waving a message form around and raving. Frost headed that way, Private Timmons in his wake, readying the cuffs.

"What in the hell is this?" Hendricks screamed. "This sonofabitch has months left in the brig. Months!"

"Well, according to this, Ed, he doesn't." The *Arizona*'s captain was looking at his own copy of the message. "Looks like someone back in Washington just pardoned the kid."

Frost approached the two men. "Who got pardoned?"

Hendricks didn't answer. The *Arizona*'s captain did. "Well, son. You did, apparently. Pardoned with orders to get your butt to DC as soon as possible."

Frost cocked his head to one side, confused by the news. A pardon?

"It's a mistake," Hendricks said. "We'll get back to the brig and I'll make some calls and…"

"No mistake, Ed." The *Arizona*'s captain pointed to the form. "Comes right from the commander at War Plans. Says right here to expedite the kid's return stateside. Even to the point of funding his flight home. No slow boat to the West Coast. They want this kid there soonest." The captain turned, looked around in the crowd, found the person he was looking for, and waved him over. "Exec, maybe you know. When's the next flight out of here?"

The *Arizona*'s executive officer checked his watch. "Leaves in about two hours. My Emmy is on the flight. Cost an arm and a leg but her pop ain't doing so well."

The *Arizona*'s captain turned to Hendricks. He was smiling and Frost had a fleeting feeling that the man was enjoying this, that he did not much like Hendricks. "Well hell, Ed. That works out just about right. My exec here can just take your boy to the airport with him." He looked over at the pile of boiler tech his sailors were retrieving from the ring. "Worth it, too. With what he did to Jorgensen over there. First fight my man ever lost."

Frost watched Hendricks, saw him looking from face to face, knew what was going through the man's mind.

He wants someone to tell him that this was all some sort of mistake. A joke. A prank. He's made five grand betting my way. Five grand in the few months since he'd found out that I could box. And with the fleet at Pearl and the smokers increasing in frequency…

But his stallion is being taken away. Sure, I'm a royal pain in the ass. To him, I'm everything that the military is not supposed to allow. Disrespectful. Insubordinate. A loner. But I'm a money-making machine. And some flag officer in Washington is stealing me away. It didn't much matter why or how.

Frost saw Hendricks glaring at him.

He grinned.

3 | Union Station

Frost checked his watch for the hundredth time.

Three hours out, he thought. Three more hours until I find out what all of this is about. Maybe.

He tried to close his eyes, tried to force himself to sleep. But it was no use. His mind would not stop racing. Would not stop reliving the odd circumstances that had placed him in this car, on this train.

From the brig to DC in forty-eight hours.

Damn.

He reached up, flipped the small toggle switch above his head, flooding his private room with a pale, golden light. He rolled to his left, his hand reaching for the canvas bag on the floor, digging in it for…

There…

He withdrew the crumpled orders, smoothed the mimeographed pages on his chest, and held them up. He read them. Again.

Expedite return of…

Report to Commander, War Plans Division…

Nothing new. No information he might have missed in the first four readings. No extraneous line of print that provided any sort of clue what this was all about. And absolutely no hint of why he, of all people, had been summoned to Washington, DC.

He stuffed the papers back into the bag. He flipped off the light and tried to force himself to rest, to enjoy the soft comfort of the thick mattress, listening to the gentle clacking of the train as it sped along through western Pennsylvania.

Could be worse, he thought. At least it's DC. They could have sent me back to the 4th Marines and that idiot, Whitehead.

Frost closed his eyes, concentrating on the gentle rocking of the car as the train sped through the night, down through the mountains and foothills of Appalachia.

———

Colonel McDonald removed a thin, wire-framed pair of reading glasses from his drooping face. He pinched his nose and rubbed his temples, praying that the dull, nagging headache would stay in the background and not erupt into something far more obnoxious.

He'd been at his desk for almost twenty-four hours straight. Catching up, mostly. Pushing paper. Solving this problem and trying to address that one. Reviewing operations orders and requisitions and bulldozing his way through the mountain of administrative duties that came with his job.

And thinking.

Looking for a way around a problem that would not go away. A problem that was, according to his watch, less than two hours away.

"Why in the hell would the general want to see Frost first?" he asked the ceiling. "What point would that serve?"

He knew the answer. Knew it for a fact.

He just didn't like it.

But he ordered you to bring Frost here, his mind argued. The man gave you a lawful order. And you have to follow those. Even if the man giving the order is a moron.

"Especially then," McDonald growled to the desk lamp, a small green and brass fixture that had once belonged to his grandfather.

A thought percolated in his mind. A lesson from the distant past, from his own time as a fresh, young second lieutenant. Rising. Bubbling. Relevant.

Salute the uniform. Not the man.

McDonald grunted, supposing that the advice applied to his present situation.

An order had been given. An order must be followed.

"And if I do that," McDonald asked himself, "what then?"

He knew the answer to that. Knew it cold.

Frost would walk out. He'd leave. One whiff of the general's cologne, maybe not even that, and Frost would say no to Jackson and Stevens and whoever the hell that third man had been.

"He'll take his discharge and leave," McDonald told the lamp.

Back to Indiana, he wondered? Or somewhere else? Where?

McDonald leaned back in his seat, cursed the general, and closed his eyes.

Such a small man, he thought. A small, petty man. Making a demand like that.

And why?

Because he's mad. He's angry. Because Frost broke his nose two years ago and he wants Frost to suffer. And because this Jackson guy had the pull to set Frost free…

McDonald's eyes popped open. He sat up. He picked through the papers on his desk, found what he was looking for, snatched the phone from its receiver, and gave directions to the operator.

The line rang. Once. Twice. A click. A soft female voice.

"Federal Trade Committee. How may I direct your call?"

McDonald smiled. "Mr. Jackson, please. It's Colonel McDonald at War Plans."

"One moment, sir."

Frost stepped onto the platform at Washington's Union Station, looking around at the marbled floors, ionic columns, and sculptures that surrounded him.

Neoclassical, his mind reported. Some half-remembered bit of information from college. He smiled, walked across the open platform, following the small, posted signs leading him toward the building's main entrance and wondering who it was that would be meeting him at the doors. The orders, he reflected, hadn't covered that in detail.

Just said I'd be picked up, he thought. Likely someone in uniform?

He looked around again and shook his head. It was possible, but unlikely. There were at least fifty people in uniform within one hundred yards of where he was now walking. Young sailors, natty in their dress whites and black neckerchiefs. Soldiers and Marines, also in dress uniforms with rows of ribbons adorning their breasts. None of them senior. And none of them appeared to be the least bit interested in him.

So, who? He pondered the question, weaving around passengers and families and small kiosks selling bags of snacks and fresh coffee and the latest newspapers.

Whoever it was would need to be…

"Captain Frost, I presume?"

Frost stopped walking, looked to his right, searched for the speaker. No one in uniform, he noted. But there was a man staring at him. A short, older man with graying hair, a brown suit, and an open paper.

"You are Captain Everett Frost? United States Marine Corps?" the man asked with one bushy eyebrow raised. "Don't much look like the photo in your record."

Frost cringed at the use of his first name—his grandfather's name—hating it as much now as he had in his youth.

The man folded the newspaper in his hands and waved to the seat beside him.

Frost nodded, then took the offered seat.

The man extended a hand. "I'm Colonel Isaac McDonald. Assistant to the Commander, War Plans."

Frost shook the man's hand, looked down at his own civilian clothes, thought to apologize for not being in uniform.

McDonald chuckled. "Don't sweat the uniform, son. As you see, I'm not wearing mine. And I wrote the orders that got you out of that brig. I know the score."

"Didn't have much time to collect my things, sir." Frost apologized anyway.

"I guess not, moving you out fast as we did." McDonald nodded. "I hear you were out boxing when the orders went through. Smokers on Battleship Row or something like that. Against some Navy snipe?"

Frost nodded. "Yes, sir."

"You win?"

"I did, sir."

A smile. "Good." McDonald coughed, checked his watch, looked around. "Now, if I was you, I'd be wondering why a bird colonel was collecting me from the train station. And in civilian clothes, no less." McDonald didn't give Frost time to respond. "Well, the short answer is that I'm not collecting you. Someone else will be along any minute to do that. I'm just babysitting."

"So, I'm not getting picked up by a full colonel, just being babysat by one?"

McDonald nodded. "I know it sounds crazy, but I have my reasons."

Frost waited for McDonald to continue. When he didn't, Frost asked, "Why am I here?"

"The folks coming here to pick you up will fill you in."

"Okay." He tried a different approach. "Why are you here?"

"Because my boss is a small-minded idiot."

"I don't understand."

"Sure, you do," McDonald said. "I've seen your record. You're a smart guy, good with logic and all that. What do your orders say? Who are you supposed to report to?"

"Your boss, I suppose. The Commander, War Plans."

McDonald nodded. "And, let me tell you, son, the Commander, War Plans Division doesn't really want you here." A pause. "More correctly, he is opposed to your being summoned here in the first place. He'd rather you continued to rot away in that jail cell back in Pearl."

Frost cocked his head, more confused now than when he'd left the train. "Why would your boss care about a single Marine in a little brig on some island in the middle of the Pacific?"

McDonald let a thin smile ease onto his face. "Let's just say you and he have had a… professional disagreement. A falling-out, so to speak. About two years back."

"I've never met the…" Frost stopped, thinking. The corners of his mouth turned down. His head shook gently. "No. It can't be…"

McDonald was watching him. "Yeah, you get it now, don't you, Captain?"

"And you're supposed to take me to him?"

"If I was the man picking you up first, yes. But I'm not. I'm just a grumpy old warhorse sitting and reading the funny pages who just happened to be here when you wandered by. So, I figured I'd sit and have a chat with you, since you're new to DC and all. Just wait with you."

"Until the folks you talked about get here?"

McDonald opened his paper, leaned back against the wooden bench, and nodded.

"And who are they?"

"Ask 'em yourself. They're heading this way."

Frost looked around, saw two men in dark suits walking toward him. Neither was smiling. Neither held a hand out.

"Captain Frost?" said the taller of the two.

Frost got up. "That's right."

"My name is Jackson. Would you come with us, please?" The man turned and began walking away.

"What's this all about?" Frost asked before he got three paces.

"We'll explain when we get to my office, Captain. Please, follow me."

Frost looked at the men. Looked at Colonel McDonald. Saw him stand.

"I'd go with them, son." He folded his paper and tucked it under an arm. "Whatever they have in store for you can't be worse than living in a jail cell. Sure as hell can't be worse than serving as some pugilist stalking horse for a trumped-up squid captain bent on making some money. Hell, you might even like whatever they have in store."

McDonald grinned, slapped Frost on the back, and walked off into the crowd. Frost looked after him, watched him disappear, and then turned to the two men in dark suits, saw them staring.

He collected his small duffel and followed the man calling himself Jackson through the building, out the doors, and into an idling car.

The drive lasted twenty minutes, the large Packard Eight weaving around light traffic and through the dizzying maze of DC side streets while the Ink Spots crooned on the radio. Ridge tried to keep his bearings, tried to focus on certain landmarks, but gave the task up halfway through the ride. He'd never been in DC before and without any sort of background or reference, tracking the landmarks did him little good.

The car pulled to a stop on a dark, tree-lined street. The men got out, leaving Frost to pop the door and exit the car on his own.

"This way," said Jackson, pointing at a small, corner building of what looked like white stone. He led the way up the steps to the door, pausing when he got there. He turned. "Captain, before we go in, there's something I need to make clear. We pulled you out of that brig in Pearl because we've got a little problem we think you can help us with." He paused. "But you gotta decide whether you're in or out. Right here. Right now." He jabbed at the heavy doors to the building with a finger. "Because once you pass these doors, anything we tell you is classified. Better than Top Secret. Meaning…"

"I know what that means," Frost said.

"Good." Jackson smiled for the first time. "Then you understand how this works. You enter. I enter. We talk over our little problem. And you leave. Whether or not you help us is immaterial. But if you don't, and you utter a single word…"

"Back to the brig?"

"You'll wish it was back to the brig," Jackson said. "Let's just leave it at that. I don't like making threats. And I don't expect you'll turn us down."

"And why is that?"

Jackson smiled in response, pulled a set of keys from a pocket. "What'll it be, Captain? You in or out?"

Frost looked up and down the street, smelled the warm, sweet air, heard a cat screech, heard a dog bark. He looked at Jackson. He looked at the other man. He shrugged.

"Hell, gentlemen. Why not?"

Jackson turned and stabbed the key into the lock. "Good boy."

4 | Uranium Club

Frost entered the office and glanced around, taking in as many details as possible. The plain, unadorned walls. The two short bookcases. The deep, worn seats. The simple but elegant desk. The warm, pungent smells of leather and paper and dust.

And something else.

Something burnt and sweet.

Pipe tobacco?

It was, he decided, a comfortable room. Or should have been. Under normal circumstances, Frost would have felt right at home in a room like this. But these weren't normal circumstances. The man calling himself Jackson pointed to a seat.

"I would ask you about your trip, son, but frankly, I don't really give a damn." He removed his suit coat, draped it over the back of the large leather chair behind the desk. "I suppose it is good manners, though."

Frost thought about the trip. The train ride from San Francisco hadn't been bad at all. Good, solid food. What his father would have called country fare. His own private room.

Even a series of hot showers along the way, a luxury that he'd been denied for most of the previous two years.

But the flight? How to describe the flight? How to describe his first time in a plane? He almost laughed. Flying was, without a doubt, the most unnatural act he'd ever performed. Sixteen hours in that contraption, vomiting every so often and praying to whatever God there might be that it stayed aloft and functioned as intended. And if it didn't? Well, he'd reflected on that possibility during the flight. It was impossible not to. Unless the damned thing exploded in mid-air, he figured he'd have had a good two minutes or so to know he was going to die as the plane fell out of the sky.

"The trip was fine, sir," Frost said.

"I suppose that's good. Considering." Jackson began rolling up his sleeves.

The door opened behind Frost. He turned to look. One of the arrivals was the second man from the train station. The other was new. Jackson introduced both.

"This here is Mr. Stevens." Jackson pointed. "You met him at the station." He turned. "This gentleman is Mr. Lamkin. Most of what you're about to hear was his idea."

Frost shook hands with the two men. Stevens was short and thick, a younger, stronger version of the colonel from the train depot. The man introduced as Lamkin was…

Average, Frost thought. Average build. Average height. Average hair. Average face. Average everything. It struck him that this man, this Mr. Lamkin, could disappear in plain sight, could be standing right and front of you and you wouldn't remember a thing about him five minutes later. Everything about him was so very…

Plain.

Except the eyes, Frost thought. The man has hard eyes. The same eyes his Marines had had. Intelligent eyes. Cool and dangerous.

"How much have you covered, Henry?" asked Stevens.

"Just the niceties. How was the trip? That kind of thing."

Stevens nodded, took the seat beside Frost, pulled a pack of cigarettes from a pocket.

"You smoke, Captain?"

Frost shook his head, looked down at his clothing.

"Gentlemen, my apologies for the attire. My uniforms…"

"Are still in the brig." Jackson waved the apology away. "We know all about that and it's no matter. You won't need 'em."

"We kind of skipped that part, sir. On the way to the airport."

Stevens lit a cigarette, put the pack away, exhaled thin wisps of blue smoke from his nostrils. "I heard our orders caught you in the middle of a boxing match."

Frost nodded. "That's correct, sir."

"You win?"

"I did, sir."

"Good. Been fighting long?"

"Since high school, sir. That and wrestling and baseball."

Stevens nodded, turned to look at Mr. Lamkin. "Greg?"

Mr. Lamkin pulled a folder from a briefcase Frost had not noticed before and tossed it onto Jackson's desk. "Been over your records, Captain. Not bad. Not bad at all. Solid academics, both in high school and at the Naval Academy. A degree in physics. Fourth in your class. Chose to be a Marine. Boxing. Wrestling. Baseball, like you said. Plus, some judo in your senior year. Combat veteran. Good marks on almost every fitness report." Lamkin let loose a sly grin at that statement. "Most impressively, you speak four languages in addition to English. French. Russian. Spanish. And German."

"Thank you, sir."

"They usually teach those languages in school in Indiana?" Stevens asked.

"No, sir," Frost said. "Only languages I took in high school were Latin and French."

"Where'd you pick up the others?" Jackson said.

"Books, mostly," Frost answered. "Plus, what some of my Marines taught me."

Stevens laughed. "No formal training in German, Spanish, or Russian and you're fluent in all three?"

"That's about the size of it, sir."

Stevens grinned, stubbed out the remains of his first cigarette, lit a second. "I'm impressed to hell, son. I have a hard enough time with one language." He looked to Mr. Lamkin. "What do you think, Greg?"

Lamkin's voice was a low, slow and drawl. Thoughtful. "I think he's perfect for the job, if he's willing."

They were watching him, Frost saw. Hitting him for reactions. Waiting for something.

Jackson leaned back in his chair. "Captain, it's probably no surprise that the Marines aren't real happy with you right now."

"I'd have to agree," Frost said.

"So, it wouldn't be much of a shock if I told you that we have some discharge papers here for you. Other than honorable. Because of that incident with the general in Shanghai." Jackson pointed to a neat pile of papers resting on the corner of his desk. "In that pile, right there."

"I expected to be discharged."

"I didn't figure it would be breaking news." Jackson stretched, leaned forward. "Seeing how you're on the way out and all, we figured we'd throw a job your way."

"What kind of job?"

Frost saw Jackson and Stevens look to Lamkin. He turned, repeated the question. "What's the job?"

Lamkin reached into his briefcase, removed a folded half-sheet of paper. "This came in over the wire a few days ago. The circumstances surrounding the transmission are largely irrelevant. Just know that the man who transmitted it is our ambassador in Berlin and the man he got the information from has our complete trust."

Lamkin handed the page over. Frost looked around the room, eyeballed each of the men, then turned his attention to the pale yellow page. He read it once, then a second time. Then he looked up.

"I don't understand," he said. "This just says that this man, Locksmith, needs to have a sit-down with someone from the embassy." He looked back down at the note, scanning the last line of handwritten text. "Something about…" Frost's voice trailed off. "I don't know. I can't read the writing here… Fur…"

"It says '*Höllenfeuer*,'" Lamkin said. "I presume you are able to translate those words."

"Hellfire?" Frost asked. He looked at the note. "This guy wants to have a conversation with someone about hellfire? Does he need a priest?"

Lamkin offered a slow smile. "No. What he wants is to talk to someone about a group called Uranverein."

Frost translated again. "Uranium Club? What the hell is that?"

Jackson and Stevens shifted in their seats, Frost saw. They looked, again, to Lamkin. Lamkin smiled. He moved away from the wall, walked to the other side of the room, to a cherry cabinet full of bottles and glasses. "Care for a drink, Captain?"

Frost said nothing. He looked at Jackson, at Stevens, and back to Lamkin, who was busying himself with a bottle of bourbon and two short, thick tumblers. He stood, held the paper out. "Gentlemen, what's going on? What is this? What's this hellfire this guy is talking about?"

Lamkin turned around with a pair of tumblers in his hands. He walked to Frost, handed him one, and jerked his chin at the seat. "Sit back down, son."

Frost took the seat. Lamkin nodded, took a drink from his glass, and moved back to his spot near the wall. "Do you know anything about Leo Szilard?"

"Who?"

"He's a scientist, Captain. A physicist, to be precise. Like you. Light years beyond you, maybe. No offense intended."

"None taken." Frost took a drink, began to respond, but was stopped when Lamkin raised a hand.

"Now, I'm not a scientist, and I'm certainly not a physicist. Most of what this Mr. Szilard talks about goes right over my head. Gibberish. Stuff I can't make heads or tails of." He sipped at his glass, smiled. "But you, Captain. You studied physics at the Academy."

Frost nodded. "Yes. But you said Uranium Club. I had very little to do with nuclear physics in school. Just the basics, really. And I still don't see what this has—"

Lamkin ignored Frost, kept talking. "So, a week ago, this Szilard fellow, he writes a letter, see? Writes a letter and hands it off to a buddy of his. The buddy reads it, signs it, and the letter makes it all the way to the Oval Office. Right to the top. Lots of technical jargon in that letter. Stuff I don't understand. Things you might. But the big view of the letter is fairly simple. These two men, this Szilard and his buddy, have convinced FDR that they can use what they're calling nuclear chain reactions to make the biggest damned bomb the world has ever seen."

Frost felt his blood run cold. He looked down at the paper in one hand. Lifted the drink in the other, put it to his lips. Felt the thick, syrupy liquor dribble past his tongue and slip down his throat. Felt the warmth as it traveled.

"Hellfire," he muttered.

"Hellfire," Lamkin repeated. "Have you heard of anything like this?"

"Not this exactly." Frost was surprised to hear the tremor in his voice. He looked at the paper again. "But something like it. Something very, very basic. Nothing more than a theory, really. Fantasy. The breaking of atoms. Using neutrons to split them, I think. Do that and…" His voice trailed off softly. He looked up. "Jesus. You think that this guy, this Locksmith, has information about what this Szilard is up to?"

"No." The response came from Jackson. "Not at all. We know exactly what Szilard and his friend are up to. This has nothing to do with them."

"Remember, Captain," said Stevens, "this message came from Berlin."

Frost's drink stopped halfway to his lips and lowered. His hand was shaking. He looked at Stevens. "Do you mean…?"

"I'm afraid so," Stevens said. "It would appear that the Nazis are working along these same lines."

"They're the ones who first made the discovery, you know," Jackson said.

"What discovery?" Frost asked.

"Fission, they're calling it," Jackson answered. "Splitting atoms. Like you said. Only it's no longer just a theory."

Frost felt his skin crawl. "Excuse me?"

"It happened while you were rotting away in that brig," Lamkin said. "A pair of German scientists figured out that you could bombard atoms with other atoms and break them apart. And when you do…"

"Energy is released," Frost said, his eyes locked on the message form in his left hand, the drink in his right forgotten. His mind shifted, racing, working to recall lessons from college, trying to calculate. "Lots of energy. A whole goddamned shitpot full. Enough to… Jesus… This might be possible." He looked up.

"Yeah," Lamkin said. "That's what the president thinks. He's gonna set this Szilard and his friend up with some funding and a committee to see what they can do. They're getting started in a couple months, from what I gather."

Frost set his drink on Jackson's desk, held the form in both hands. "But you think that this hellfire is the same thing, don't you? And you need someone to go talk to this Locksmith."

"That is," Jackson said, "exactly what we need."

Frost lifted his head, looked at Jackson. "Why me?"

Jackson pointed to Lamkin. Frost turned to look at him.

"You have the educational background we need for something like this. Your record says that you are highly intelligent, and you have that degree in physics."

"That's true of thousands of others," Frost argued. "Why me? Why pick a guy even the Marines don't want?"

"That's simple." Lamkin smiled. "And you're right. There are thousands of folks around the country who could have this conversation. Mostly in academia. Professors and researchers. Men who would work quite well if the circumstances were a bit, ah, softer."

"Softer?"

Lamkin leaned forward, reached out, and took the note from Frost. He looked down at it. "Captain, if the Nazis are working on this, then conversations about it are going to be guarded fiercely. This is not going to be a conversation in the local *gasthaus*. And the people protecting information like this are not going to be gentle." He looked at Frost. "We need someone who can have this conversation, yes. But we also need someone who can handle himself if the going gets, shall we say, rough."

5 | Unit 12

"Who are you?" Frost addressed his question to Jackson, the man who appeared to be running the show.

"Officially? Well, as far as anyone outside these four walls is concerned, we are the Federal Trade Committee," Jackson replied, lighting a cigarette. He pointed to the other men in the room. "Mr. Stevens here is my chief of staff, keeps me organized and whatnot. The shadowy fella against the wall there is Mr. Lamkin. He is our operations officer. Handles the day-to-day details."

Frost looked at each man in turn, nodded. "I'm going to go out on a limb and say that you gentlemen have little or nothing to do with trade. Unofficially or otherwise."

Jackson chuckled. "Well, now, that depends."

"On what?"

"On what's being traded," Stevens answered.

Cute, Frost thought. Real cute. He looked around the room, thought about the short briefing he'd received. "Intel?"

Jackson nodded. "Unofficially, we're known, when we're known at all, as Unit Twelve." He let his words hang in the thick, smoky air. "Intelligence collection, analysis, and, if necessary, operations. Working directly for State." A pause.

"More specifically, we work directly for the Secretary of State, who gets his marching orders from FDR."

"Like a personal shotgun?" Frost asked.

"We try to avoid that," Lamkin said. "Whenever possible."

Frost thought for a moment. "Unit Twelve? Does that—"

Jackson stopped the question with a raised hand. "No, it doesn't. We are the only unit. No Units One or Two. Just us." He pointed at Lamkin. "His idea. And not a bad one, at that. If word ever gets out about us, beyond the people who are authorized to know, it might cause some confusion. At the very least, it should force the other side to waste time worrying about the eleven non-existent teams."

Frost allowed a small, almost imperceptible smile to cross his face. It was clever, he thought. Almost too clever. He remained silent for a good, long while, his mind tumbling over the information he'd been given, knowing that the men surrounding him were waiting for an answer. Waiting for a yes or no.

And if you say no? What then? What will they do with you? Back to Hawaii? Back to the brig? Back to Hendricks? Jackson's words came back to him. A threat, whether he called it that or not. The brig would be the least of your problems.

"Captain?"

Frost looked up, turned, saw Jackson watching him.

"I know what you're thinking. There's something you should know. Something I should make clear. If you choose not to help us, you will be returned to the brig at Pearl Harbor to serve the remainder of your term before the discharge from the Marine Corps will be enforced."

Frost pondered the thought, weighed it. Calculating. Several months left in the brig. Plus five days for the thing with Corporal Parks. Versus what? And how did that fit with Jackson's earlier warning?

"I should also point out that Captain Hendricks is currently preparing charges of attempted murder on the off chance that you are somehow returned to his custody. It is our understanding that you had a few months left in the brig the morning the orders went out to send you here. But…" Jackson's voice drifted off as his hands went to work, shuffling through the pile of papers. He seized a single sheet, pulled it from the pile. "Apparently there was an incident the morning the orders were sent. An assault on a Corporal Parks with," he looked up at Frost, "his own baton? Do I have that right?"

Frost thought he saw the smallest hint of a smile creep onto Lamkin's face. He nodded. "Yes, sir. That's right."

"You beat up one of the guards with his own billy club?" Stevens asked.

"I did, sir."

"Why?"

Frost looked at Lamkin, saw that the man was most definitely smiling. "Well, sir. He came into the cell to tune me up, if you know what I mean. So, I took his toy away."

"Just like that?" Jackson asked. He looked at Frost more closely. "Not a scratch on you."

Frost shrugged. "Him or me, sir."

Jackson grinned, put the form aside. "I suppose you know that an attempted murder charge would keep you in that cell for the better part of the next decade. Might even end with you dangling at the end of a few yards of government-procured rope. Yes?"

"I know, sir," Frost agreed. He thought for a few seconds more and stood. "Well, gentlemen, I'm not exactly looking forward to ten more years in the brig, so…"

"You're in?" Jackson asked.

"I'm in."

Jackson stood, crushed the butt of his cigarette out in a thick glass ashtray. He extended his hand. "Good. Mr. Lamkin there will take it from here. Get you sorted and fitted out."

Frost took the hand, shook it. "Fitted out?"

Stevens stood from his chair. "Hell yes, son. We're sending you to Europe. Right into the cultural heart of Nazi Germany. Can't have you showing up there looking like some bum we just picked up at a local prison."

"Even if that's precisely what we did," Stevens offered.

Frost looked down at his clothes, pulled at the lapels of his ill-fitting suit, wondered just where in the world these clothes had come from. Where the exec from the USS *Arizona* had picked them up.

Stevens slapped Frost on the shoulder, turned him toward the door, where Lamkin was waiting. "One thing about the Nazis—they love things to look proper. To look the part. You head on out with Mr. Lamkin and he'll fix you up. Clothes. Passports. Money. Visas. Travel arrangements."

"A sidearm?" Frost asked.

"Not at this end," said Lamkin. "We'll have something for you when you land in Europe."

Stevens grinned. "Trust me, kid. When Lamkin is done with you, you'll feel like a million bucks."

Frost followed Lamkin through the building to a small office near the back of the house. He took an offered seat and watched as Lamkin pulled a large envelope from his desk.

"Well, then," Lamkin said, drawing a thick stack of papers and documents from the envelope, "I guess we'd better get started."

———

Two floors above Frost, in a small, disused closet in the building's attic, a thin, wiry man pulled a set of headphones from his ears. He'd been listening for nearly thirty minutes and his ears were sore from the way the phones pressed against them. He switched off the radio set he'd been using, disconnected the battery, and carried everything out of the closet. He turned the corner, careful to step on the thick rafters, knelt, and buried the collection of gear in a box hidden beneath two layers of insulation. Finished, he made his way to the stairs at the opposite end of the attic, collecting a pile of random records from a box stowed nearby, and worked his way down the steep incline. As he made his way to his office, the man congratulated himself for what he'd accomplished and began composing an urgent message for his contact at the German Embassy.

Three minutes later, the man from the attic stepped into his office, locked the records in his desk, and collected his coat.

"I'm heading out for an early lunch," he told his secretary. "Want anything?"

The young woman smiled, shook her head, and turned her attention back to her typewriter.

Once outside the building, the man donned his coat and walked three blocks north before turning east. There was a new delicatessen that he'd been meaning to try down that way.

More importantly, there was a pharmacy on the way with a pay phone in the back.

Eight blocks later, the man entered the phone booth in the rear of the pharmacy and shut the hinged door. He picked up the receiver, directed the operator to connect him to a memorized number, and waited.

The line rang once. Twice. And was picked up.

"Hello," said a voice with a thick accent.

"Yes," said the man from the attic, "is this Mr. Thompson?"

The line remained silent for five seconds. Ten.

"I'm sorry, sir," said the voice. "Mr. Thompson has been transferred."

"Back to the home office?"

"Yes, sir," said the voice. "Is there something I can help you with?"

This guy's English is very good, thought the man from the attic. Even with the accent. "Yes, maybe you can. I met with Mr. Thompson several months back, during a reception at the Mayflower. It was in April, I think. April the thirteenth. About a renovation project. His fireplace, you see."

"I see," said the voice. "I can pass along a message if you like."

"That would be helpful. Thank you." The man from the attic rang off and left the booth, heading across the street to the delicatessen. A Reuben, he thought, would hit the spot.

Fifteen blocks away, the man who'd taken down a message about Mr. Thompson's fireplace project reviewed the information he'd just been given, matching up the words and phrases with meanings he'd memorized. He replaced the handset for his phone, left his office, and strode briskly along the hall, around a corner, and down the stairs leading to the basement. There, he found the third door on the left, knocked, and entered when a small light above the door turned green.

A large, heavyset man sat behind a small desk. He had a short neck and a thick, bald head, wide shoulders, and huge, meaty hands. He looked up.

"Yes, Gertler. What is it?"

Gertler swallowed hard, worked to keep from trembling. "A call, Herr Strauss. From our contact on Belmont Road in Kalorama."

Strauss's head rose slowly at the mention of the address. "Really?"

"Yes, Herr Strauss. And quite important." Gertler tried to keep his eyes on the wall behind Strauss, tried to avoid staring at the man's face, at the scar tissue covering the left side of the head.

"Go on," Strauss ordered.

"Our contact says that they are sending a man to Berlin, Herr Strauss. Presumably to collect information from someone there." Gertler's voice shook.

Strauss cocked his head to one side. "That's not exactly urgent, Gertler. The Americans like to send spies everywhere. Their General Washington started the practice, I think. During their rebellion against the English—"

"Yes, Herr Strauss," Gertler interrupted.

Strauss's eyes flared; the face reddened. Gertler felt his pulse race, felt beads of icy sweat form on his forehead and at his collar.

"My apologies, Herr Strauss," Gertler said. "The contact from Belmont Road did pass on that the spy is being sent to gather information on Project Hellfire. With respect, that is one of the priority code words."

"Hellfire? Are you certain?"

"Yes, Herr Strauss. Quite certain."

Gertler watched Strauss, saw the man's face go blank for several moments. Then the change came. The eyes widened. He leaned into his desk, his large hands shuffling through stacks of documents. He seized one folder, yanked it from its pile. Opened it. Read. Gertler saw Strauss's eyes narrow, saw the man's brow furrow. Finally, he looked up.

"Thank you, Herr Gertler. You are dismissed," Strauss said, his voice sharp, stressed.

Gertler saluted, his right arm forward and up. He turned on his heels, walked three paces to the door, and grabbed hold of the knob.

"Wait," commanded Strauss, "Did your contact say anything else? When this spy is to leave? Where he is now?"

Gertler cursed himself. How had he forgotten that? He turned back. "Nothing about leaving, Herr Strauss. But he is staying at the Mayflower Hotel. Suite four-thirteen."

"You are certain?"

Gertler nodded. "My contact told me that he met Mr. Thompson about a fireplace project at the Mayflower on April thirteenth."

"Very good," Strauss looked down at his folder. "Dismissed."

Gertler left the room as quickly as possible.

Behind him, in the office, Colonel Frederich Strauss read the information on the back page of the folder once. Then a second time. He shook his head, muttering.

Eliminate at first available opportunity.

Why? He wondered. Wouldn't it be preferable to follow a spy? To see whom, he visits? Who he gains assistance from?

Strauss's eyes traveled back down to the folder, to the first line on the last page.

By order of the Führer.

Strauss closed the folder and picked up his phone. He placed two calls. The first one went to the ambassador's office, to schedule a meeting over lunch. The second was routed to a house in Bethesda, Maryland.

The line rang twice before a young woman answered.

"This is Strauss. Tell Bauer to come see me. I have a job for him."

Frost stepped into room 413 at the Mayflower Hotel seven hours after agreeing to work for Henry Jackson and Unit 12. He was followed by Mr. Lamkin and the bellboy they had enlisted to carry Frost's new suitcases.

The room was, by a long stretch, the most luxurious set of sleeping quarters Frost had ever seen. To his left, a massive four-poster bed dominated the room, covered with a thick, coffee-colored comforter and an arrangement of downy pillows in various shades of blue satin. Thin, wispy curtains surrounded the bed, tied off to the posts with arm-length ropes of deep gold. To the right of the door, Frost found the sitting area, complete with a pair of tufted wingbacks in burgundy velvet and a low, rich cherry coffee table in front of a fireplace faced in pristine Italian marble.

"Hope you like the place," Lamkin said, dismissing the bellboy with a wave and a folded wad of banknotes. "Best we could arrange on short notice."

Frost started to say something, but caught the barely hidden grin on Lamkin's face. He smiled back.

"Sure beats staying in the brig."

Lamkin grunted. "Bet it does." He checked his watch. "They'll be bringing you chow in a few minutes. Eat. Get cleaned up. Try to relax and get some rest. I'll be back at six in the morning to escort you to the airport."

Frost tried not to react to that news and failed.

Lamkin chuckled. "Not a fan of air travel?"

Frost shook his head. A fan? Definitely not. Not even remotely.

"Well," Lamkin went on. "Can't say I blame you. I don't much like flying myself. Could have shipped you over on a liner, but there's just no time for that."

"It's fine," Frost lied. "It's just…"

"Unnatural." Lamkin raised an eyebrow. "Yeah, I said the same thing. I don't trust what I can't see, and I can't see what's keeping the plane up. Different on a boat. You can see the water. And the fall isn't so damned far." He turned, walked to the door, stopped, looked back. "Still got that phone number I gave you?"

Frost reached into a pocket, withdrew a thin scrap of paper and held it up.

"Good," Lamkin said. "Memorize it and burn it." He pointed at the paper. "That number is the link between you and my office. You don't keep something like that just lying around." He tapped the side of his head. "Keep it in here. Use it only if you need it. Any questions?"

"If I need it, who do I say I am?"

Lamkin smiled. "You're just you, kid. Everett Frost. Private citizen. Whoever answers that phone will recognize your name. And they'll find me. No matter where I am or what I'm doing."

"Fair," Frost judged. "Do me a favor?"

"What's that?"

"Let's not use my first name."

Lamkin grinned. "Sure, kid. What'll it be? Frost? Ridge?"

"Frost is fine."

"Don't like your first name?"

"Not really."

"Mine's Aloysius. I can understand."

"Aloysius?"

Lamkin winced, nodding. "Greg. I answer to Greg."

"Greg it is."

Lamkin checked his watch again, looked at Frost. "Remember, Frost. Your cover is your real life. Mostly. The Corps just booted you. You're angry or disgruntled or whatever. Mistreated. Ill-used. Not happy with the service and not happy with America."

"And my reason for heading to Berlin?"

"You like the Nazis," Lamkin said. "Feel like they've got it. On the right track."

"Felt the call to return to the Fatherland?" Frost asked.

"Something like that," Lamkin agreed. He turned to the door, grabbed the knob.

And twisted.

6 | Door Kickers

The door to the suite exploded inward, cracking and splintering on its hinges. Smoke roiled. Fragments whispered. Bomb, Frost's mind reported. He shifted to his left, ducked behind one of the wingback chairs, lost sight of Lamkin behind the crashing door.

Two men rushed into the room, pistols in hand, high and spitting. Rounds raced past Frost, slammed into the plaster behind him. Around the edge of the chair, Frost saw one gunman clearing the bed side of the room. Saw him turning right, toward the seating area and the chair where Frost crouched. Frost cursed, turned, looking for anything that…

There!

His hand shot out, latched onto the cast iron poker for the fireplace, pulled it close. He crouched lower, moved deeper into the corner. Wedged his back against the wall. He lifted his feet, placed them on the back of the chair, trying to gauge where the center of gravity would be.

Through the din echoing in his ears, he heard the man shuffling closer. Saw the tip of the gun over the corner of the chair.

Frost clutched the poker tight, tensed his legs, braced his back, and kicked. Hard.

The heavy chair vaulted forward, slammed into the gunman, tripping him, veering the gun away, toward the window to Frost's right.

Frost launched to his feet, swinging the poker around like a baseball bat. It slammed into the man, striking the gun hand as the man worked to keep his balance and direct the weapon at this unexpected threat. The small pistol fell, bounced on the carpet, as its owner tried to stabilize himself. Frost reversed his swing, coming out of the room's corner and bashing the man on his right shoulder. The man twisted sideways, falling away from the blow, rolling toward the windows, onto his back. Frost chased him, swinging the poker overhand, bringing it down with all the violence he could muster.

The gunman caught the poker, wrapped his hands around the end, and pulled. Frost felt himself being yanked forward, let the poker go, and kicked at the prone man, crowding him into the tight space between the bed and the exterior wall. To his left, Frost heard the gunshots stop, heard a crash. He started to turn, but fought the urge, forced himself to focus on the threat at his feet and not the one at the other end of the room.

The man with the poker tried to sit up, to squeeze out of the confined space between the bedframe and the plaster wall. Frost towered over him, launching a series of kicks at any part of the man's body he could get to while he tried to think of a way to finish the fight. The poker came slicing toward him, an overhand swing from the man pinched on the floor. Frost swatted it aside with his left forearm, felt a brief, searing pain along the bone on the underside of his arm. He lashed out with his foot, kicked the man's feet aside, and launched himself closer, reaching for the collar of the man's buttoned shirt.

Frost got hold of the collar in his left hand, used his side to pin the arms waving the poker down. He bunched the collar up and twisted. The man on the floor let go of the poker. His hands shot up, first to his own neck, then to Frost's. Frost pulled the hands away, swatted at them, grabbed the fingers, squeezed, and twisted. The legs under him tried to kick. Tried to shove. Tried to dig in, to gain purchase, to create space to maneuver. Frost scooted closer, still twisting the collar. The man's face changed color. First red. Then a purplish hue. He tried to move his hands back to his own neck, to pick and pull at Frost's grip. Frost let his grip on the hands loosen, reached one arm back, and slammed his fist into the oxygen-deprived face. Once. Twice. A third time.

Frost felt the body under him go limp. He pushed himself up, breathing hard. Sweating. He scanned the room. Saw Lamkin was down. Saw the other gunman lifting his pistol. Frost moved quickly, climbing onto the bed, grabbing the loose poker as he went. He threw himself at the second gunman, swinging the poker around in a vicious arc as the man's finger depressed the trigger.

The shot rang out, loud, reverberating.

Lamkin grunted.

The poker slammed into the side of the gunman's head with a sickening, wet thud. Blood sprayed, crimson droplets catapulting through the air.

The man dropped.

Frost looked at him, saw the massive wound the poker had caused. Saw the blood pooling around the shattered skull.

He looked to Lamkin. Saw him crouched against the foyer wall. Saw a reddish stain spreading across his right shoulder. Saw that he was pale as a ghost.

Frost grabbed a towel from the bathroom, wedged it against Lamkin's shoulder, helped him press it in place. Lamkin started to scream, ground his teeth together.

"Hold this here for a second," Frost ordered.

Lamkin nodded, his jaws shut tight against the pain.

Frost moved to the first gunman, dragged the unconscious body from behind the bed. He yanked one of the gold ropes from the bed post and tied the man's feet. He yanked a second rope loose and tied the man's hands. He used a third rope to tie the first two ropes to each other. Satisfied, he stood erect. He looked around the sitting area, found the first gunman's pistol, collected it, and tucked it in the back waistband of his pants. He moved back to Lamkin's man, collected that gun, and pocketed it before kneeling in front of Lamkin.

"How bad?"

"Hurts like hell," Lamkin growled, turned his head away from the wound. "I'll live."

"What do I do?"

Lamkin looked at the dead gunman in front of him, turned his head gingerly to look at the trussed gunman.

"Search 'em. Pockets. Wallets." Lamkin paused, swore. "Anything you can find."

"And then?"

"Still got that number?" Lamkin groaned. Frost nodded. "Call it."

Frost looked up when the curtains to his treatment room rustled, felt his sore muscles tense.

"Hey, kid." Jackson entered the room ahead of a nurse.

"Sir." Frost relaxed.

"Your hands, sir," interrupted the nurse, a tall, willowy woman with just the tiniest bit of gray at the temples.

Frost held his hands out. The nurse took them gently, checking the left first, then the right, inspecting the damage. "This isn't too, bad, Mr. Frost. Does it hurt?"

Frost shook his head as the nurse began cleaning and wrapping the abrasions on his knuckles. His forearm, where the poker had struck, had already been examined and wrapped. He looked to Jackson.

"How is he?" he asked, meaning Lamkin.

Jackson pulled a chair away from the wall and fell into it. "He'll be fine. Through and through, mostly. Lucky. They were wheeling him into surgery when I left. Getting him all sewn back together." He leaned forward in the chair. "Greg tells me you did well."

Frost grunted. "Know what it was about?"

Jackson shook his head. "No idea. No identification on either man. The wallets you pulled had nothing in them but some loose cash. We could have everything fingerprinted, send it over to Hoover's boys, but that's probably a dead end."

"Why's that?" Frost winced when the nurse adjusted the wrap on his right hand.

Jackson ran a hand through his hair, rubbed his temples. "Too time-consuming and, unless I'm way off the mark, these boys won't have prints in ol' J. Edgar's files." He shook his head. "No, we'll have to wait until the one fellow wakes up.

Then we'll sit down and have a chat with him, see if he feels like talking."

"He's still out?"

A low, amused chuckle escaped from Jackson. "Oh yes. The doctors tell me you did quite a number on him. Two skull fractures. Front and back."

"Sorry," Frost said. "Any chance this was random? Two guys see Greg and me checking in and decide to rob us? Something like that?"

Jackson shook his head. "It's possible, but unlikely. Folks who do that kind of thing usually like to keep things nice and quiet and civil. They knock on the door, you open it, and there's a gun in your face and a demand. Blowing the door off the hinges with small, explosive charges and rolling in with guns blazing probably isn't the greatest business model for a common thief. Brings too much attention."

The nurse finished treating Frost's hands, collected her things, and departed, pulling the curtain as she went. Jackson, Frost noticed, followed her with his eyes, even leaning around the curtain to get a better view. When he looked back at Frost, he smiled.

"Isn't she a little old for you?" Frost asked.

Jackson shrugged. "Probably not. I'm a hell of a lot older than I look."

Frost shook his head and flexed his fingers in the wrappings. "Well, what happens now?"

Jackson stood, rolled his neck. "I have your things in the trunk of my car. You and I are going back to the office. You can grab some sleep there, in one of the empty rooms. In a few hours, I'll take you to the airport myself."

"And if you get anything from the guy I knocked unconscious?"

Jackson pulled the curtain to the side and waved Frost out of the treatment room. "I'll get word to you through channels."

———

Colonel Strauss picked up the phone on his desk and listened to the voice on the other end speak for two minutes, his face reddening the whole time.

"And where," Strauss finally asked, "is the other?"

"He is in the hospital, Herr Strauss. Unconscious and under guard."

"Will he talk?"

"It is possible," the voice said. "It is always possible."

"Can we get to him?"

"I can make inquiries, Herr Strauss."

"Good. Do that," Strauss ordered. "And the targets?"

"One, Lamkin, just got out of surgery. A simple bullet wound. He is expected to recover fully." The voice paused, then continued, timidly. "The second has disappeared. We lost him leaving the hospital."

Of course you did, Strauss thought. Imbeciles. What I would pay for competent officers…

Strauss disconnected the call and placed another. The phone rang only once.

"Hello?"

"Bauer, this is Strauss. I want this other man found. Check the airport. Passenger terminals. Check under your own beds.

But I want him found and I want him eliminated. By order of the Führer."

"I understand, Herr Strauss."

"And Bauer?"

"Yes?"

"No more failures."

The line went dead.

7 | Ewa

Nearly a full day later, Frost sat in a car at the entrance to Paris's Gare du Nord. He was exhausted. He hadn't slept a wink on the transoceanic flight, his second in less than a week. The memory of the assault at the Mayflower and his recently developed fear of flying were fresh and occupying a rather large amount of space in his mind. The driver, a smooth, refined-looking man Frost guessed to be in his late thirties, and who had identified himself only as Henry's man, handed over an unsealed envelope. Frost pulled the flap back and peered inside.

Tickets, he saw. And a healthy sheaf of banknotes. Nearly two thousand dollars, by his quick count.

"From Henry," the man said. "Should be enough there to get you settled in Berlin. You'll be able to exchange it when you get there. Any bank will take care of that."

Frost thanked the man, tucked the envelope in an inside pocket, and reached for the door handle. Outside his window, he saw a porter approaching the car, nearly invisible against the dark morning sky in his blue uniform and rounded hat.

The driver grabbed his arm. "One more thing."

Frost looked at him, saw him glance furtively around.

"Something in the glove box for you. Henry said it might come in handy."

Frost punched the button to open the glove box, watched the lid drop down. He smiled, stuck his hand in, and withdrew the Colt 1911–model pistol. He hefted it, felt the familiar bulge of the honey-colored wood grips. Detected the faint but pungent scent of cleaning oil. He lowered the weapon below the car's dash, ejected the magazine, caught it, saw that it was full. He inched the slide back, saw a brief glint of brass in the chamber. Loaded, he thought, slipping the magazine back into place.

"Couple of spares in the box there. And a cleaning kit," the driver said. "Plus a silencer."

Frost pulled the objects from the glove box. He screwed the silencer onto the end of the barrel and hefted the weapon again, feeling the slight shift in balance.

Not bad, he thought. He leaned forward, slipping the pistol into the back of his waistband. It would be a bit awkward, he reflected, but it would suffice for the present. He stuffed the spare magazines and kit into the suitcase on the seat beside him and snapped the lid shut as the porter reached for the car door. Frost waved him off and opened the door himself, dragging the suitcase out with him. He shut the door, turned, thought of something, and turned back. The driver leaned over and rolled the window down.

"Yeah?"

"Any word from Henry? Anything about the guy we put in the hospital?"

The man blinked, hard. Frost saw it and cocked his head. "What?"

"Aw, hell," he said. "Thought you already knew."

"Thought I knew what?" Frost asked, the hairs on the back of his neck rising.

"That guy never woke up," the driver said. "Died just before you got on the plane."

"What? How?"

"Hell, bud. I don't know. I'm no doctor. Just got word he died. Sort of as an aside. One of those throw-away comments, you know? When you're talking to someone and they just kind of veer off topic for a moment."

"Shit."

"Shit's right, bud. Watch your ass." The man grinned, rolled up the window, and edged the car away from the curb. Frost watched him go.

"Bonjour, monsieur," said the porter. "Bienvenue à la Gare du Nord. Quel train rencontrez-vous?"

Frost handed over the small suitcase, pointed to the larger one on the ground at his feet. He checked his tickets. "Nord Express," Frost said. "Seven-fifteen."

"Ah, tres bien, monsieur." The porter collected the second bag. "S'il vous plaît, suivez-moi."

Frost followed the porter into the station.

———

Forty yards from where Frost had exited his car, a man in a dark suit with a fedora pulled low on his brow stood from his spot on a wooden bench and made a great show of folding his paper. He followed Frost and the porter through the station to the platform where hundreds of people were busy waiting to board the seven-fifteen luxury streamliner to Berlin.

He checked his watch, saw that he had twenty minutes before the train was due for departure. He walked briskly to a nearby counter, purchased a ticket for one of the coach cars, and then headed to a bank of telephone booths along the platform's rear wall.

He entered an empty booth, lifted the receiver, and placed his call.

An hour later, after a meal of eggs cooked over easy with plenty of salt and pepper and butter, toast, jam, fresh orange juice, and black coffee, Frost stepped into his private cabin, careful to shut the door firmly behind him. He engaged the lock, turned around, and surveyed the room.

To his left, near to his broad shoulders, was the small lavatory with its toilet, sink, and an impossibly cramped-looking shower. Directly ahead of him was a sitting area, no more than a bench seat, he saw, but a plush one with thick cushions and access to a fold-away desk. To his right, Frost noted, the porter had already taken the liberty of pulling down the bed. Frost pressed his hand into the soft maroon blanket and felt the easy give. He grinned, thinking already about sleep. Desiring it. Needing the time to let his body switch off and rest.

And this is just the ticket, he thought. A thick, comfortable bed with clean sheets. The lilting seduction of the arrangement backed by the metronomic and orchestral clicking of the train's wheels against the rails.

Yes, he thought, looking around again. This would do nicely. A far cry from his brig cell in Pearl.

But first, there was another matter to attend to.

Frost looked to his right, saw the suitcases resting in a small cubby at the head of the bed. He selected the smaller one, hefted it onto the mattress, and laid it flat. He popped the locks on both sides, opened the lid, and dug his hand into the back, down beneath the new clothes neatly folded inside. His hand found what he was looking for, and he pulled all three objects free. He turned back to the door, saw that he'd only need two.

Frost dropped one of the wooden wedges to the floor and used his foot to shove it into place along the bottom of the door's frame. In his head, he heard Henry Jackson's advice ringing.

"Given what happened at the hotel, use these wedges in the doors to your cabin. Same when you get to Berlin. Use 'em there, too. Won't actually keep someone from opening the door, but it'll slow 'em down long enough for you to put a bullet right between their eyes when you finally see 'em."

Frost took the second wedge, placed it in the groove at the top of the door's frame, and pushed it tight with the butt of his hand. He checked his work, decided it would do, and tossed the third wedge back into the suitcase.

He removed his jacket and necktie and hung both on a hook screwed into the cabin's door. He removed the pistol from his waistband, unfolded the desk from the well in the forward bulkhead, and set the pistol on it.

Frost looked around the room, nodded to himself, and stretched out on the bed. He reached out with his right hand, snapped off the lights, and let the gentle rocking of the cabin lull him to sleep.

———

The man from the train station checked his watch, rose, and headed aft to the back of his car. He passed through the doors from his car to the next, and so on, until he reached the sleeper cars. He walked through the first car and halfway down the second before stopping. He let his hand fall to the handle of a door on the right side of the car. He twisted the knob slowly, gingerly, quietly, until he was certain the tumbler had disengaged from the frame. He pushed softly, felt the resistance of the deadbolt.

Locked, he thought.

Not that you would do anything if it wasn't, he reminded himself.

The man checked his watch.

Four hours to the next stop. There, he would gain three men. Three men to help him observe the target.

Just observe. Watch him and report. Nothing else.

Those were the orders and he was happy with them. He was, he thought, too old for much else.

The man let the door handle rotate back into place. He walked back forward to his seat, lighting a cigarette on the way and wondering who the target was and why he needed watching.

Frost woke in time for dinner. He stripped off the clothing he'd traveled and slept in and washed as best he could in the tiny shower. He toweled off in the cool air of the cabin and put on fresh clothing from the larger of the two suitcases. Good, comfortable clothes. A pair of dark blue pants, nicely tailored and fitted by a man Greg Lamkin had recommended. A plain white, cotton dress shirt with a stiff collar went on under a single-breasted suit coat that appeared no worse for wear after having been folded away in a suitcase for the better part of thirty-six hours. A thin leather belt in black, the same black shoes he'd been wearing since leaving Washington, and a pair of fashionable argyle socks finished off the ensemble.

Frost ran his hands over the bed, smoothing the blanket and sheets into something he considered inspection ready, a habit drilled into him during his time in the Marine Corps. He hefted the small valise onto the bed, opened it, and withdrew one of the spare magazines for his pistol.

He tucked the pistol into the rear of his waistband, dropped the spare magazine into an inside pocket of his suit coat, and checked himself in the mirror.

The clothes fitted him well, he saw. And the sleep had done him some good. But there were still bags under his eyes and he still looked like someone who'd had a very long past few days.

Nothing to be done about that, Frost judged. He shrugged, pulled the wedges from the cabin door, stowed them in the suitcase, and headed for the dining car, wondering what offerings would be available for supper.

———

The man from Paris looked up as the door to the dining car opened. He watched his target enter, saw him speak to the maître d', and followed him with his eyes as he was led to a table at the far end of the car. The man picked up his glass of wine, tossed off its contents, waved to the waiter, and ordered a second bottle.

"He's here," the man said to one of his recently arrived accomplices. "Far corner. Alone."

"Doing anything?" the new man asked without turning. He lifted his fork to his mouth, eyed the food stuck on the tines, and made a silent wish for good, solid German food instead of whatever it was his partner had ordered on his behalf.

"Nein. Er sitzt einfach da," said the man who'd boarded the train in Paris. "Just sitting and waiting and reading the menu."

The door to the compartment opened again and the man from Paris turned. A young woman. he saw. Mid-twenties. Lithe. Short, blonde curls. Lovely figure wrapped in a chocolate tweed skirt and a robin's-egg blue linen shirt with a high, bowed collar.

The woman smiled at him, turned to the maître d', and asked for a seat. The man turned, looked around, and asked the woman to wait. He headed to the far end of the car, spoke briefly to the target, who turned and nodded. The maître d' returned to the woman.

"Suivez-moi, mademoiselle," he said, leading the way to the target's table.

The man from Paris lifted his glass. "Was is das?"

The second man looked up from his plate, crooked an eyebrow high on his balding head. "Was?"

"Er hat Gesellschaft. Eine frau," the man from Paris said, jerking his chin at the far corner of the car. "Pretty one, too."

The second man poked at his food without turning around. "Berlin said nothing about a second target." He put his fork down, his face twisted into a mask of frustration that the man from Paris found amusing. "What the hell am I eating?"

The man from Paris chuckled, a low, amused grunting sound. "Quiche Lorraine. A tart. Gruyere, eggs, bacon. And the flaky crust." He leaned forward. "What? You don't like it?"

"I prefer something else. Something simpler," said the second man. He looked down at his food. "This is too…" His voice trailed off. "You've been in France for far too long, friend."

"Philistine," said the man from Paris, stuffing another bite into his mouth. He chewed and swallowed and checked his watch. "Thirty minutes to the next stop." He let his eyes drift to the far corner, where the target, the woman, and the maître d' were talking. "Forty-five-minute stop. We'll report in there."

———

Frost stood awkwardly when the woman and the maître d' approached the table. His greeting came out in English, nearly a stutter. "Good evening, ma'am."

"Apologies, monsieur," said the maître d', "but this is the only table in the entire car that isn't completely full."

"It's no problem," Frost said, motioning to the seat opposite his own. His voice was low and shaking. Nervous.

The woman smiled and eased herself into the offered seat. The maître d' apologized again, produced a menu, and departed with the woman's drink order.

Frost wedged himself back into his seat.

"I am sorry to impose," the woman said, her English tinged by an accent Frost couldn't place. German, he was sure. But muddled somehow. And something else. A slight wavering.

She was pretty, he thought. Almost as tall as he was, slim and lithe. Short, blonde curls. Well dressed. Bright eyes of pale blue that nearly matched her shirt. A wide smile. And a perfect little button of a nose, upturned ever so slightly at the tip.

Frost felt his heart rate rise, felt his neck and ears begin to flush. Knew that he needed to say something. Anything. His brain screamed at him to speak, and he cursed his innate bashfulness. Wrestling? Fine. Boxing? Even better. Cannon fire? No problem. Gunfire? Piece of cake. But put a woman in front of me and have her speak, and all of a sudden, my damned brain stops functioning.

It was, unfortunately, he thought, nothing new. He became clumsy and awkward when he spoke to women. When he was around women. When he was within fifty yards of a woman.

His mind flashed backward through time. To a dance at his school. He'd spent two hours there, leaning against the wall and praying that no one would ask him to dance. And then Julie Gardner had found him. Had asked him to waltz. He'd frozen at first. Paralyzed. But then she'd asked if he was okay. And that was when his stomach had lurched. And roiled. And ejected both helpings of his mother's pot roast onto Julie Gardner's brand-new shoes.

"Sir, are you alright?"

Frost felt his face flush. She was smiling at him. Say something, his mind screamed. Speak, you idiot. Speak!

He nodded.

"Are you sure that this is okay?" She started to move, to shift to the edge of the seat, the smile fading and her brow knitting. "Because I can wait to eat, or ask the maître d' for…"

"It's okay," Frost finally spit the words out. "I just... I get..." He felt his stomach roll and was immediately happy that there was nothing in it yet.

She paused, half out of the seat. She looked at him and the smile started to return. She ran a hand through the left side of her hair, brushing it back, exposing an ear that was bright crimson. Her eyes glittered. She moved back into the seat.

"Me too," she said. "I get so nervous around..." Her voice drifted. "I mean, I..."

Frost let loose a wide grin, felt the color recede. "Hi."

Dear God, his mind thought. Here you are on a luxurious trip across Europe. You have nice clothes, plenty of cash. You're a combat Marine. And the best you can do is grin like an idiot and say hi?

Brilliant, Ridge. Fucking brilliant.

Frost looked at the woman across from him. She stared back at him, offered a sheepish half-wave with one hand, and let loose her own wide, embarrassed smile.

"Hi. I'm Ewa. Ewa Fischer."

8 | Gerald

Frost and Ewa progressed through their meals slowly and with relish. His was a succulent roast beef surrounded by an assortment of fresh, crisp vegetables. Hers was a fine coq au vin. They picked their way through each course, talked, and sipped at glasses of a dark and meaty '24 claret recommended by the waiter. Both declined dessert, opting instead for fresh cups of rich, black coffee.

"So," Frost asked, "you're living in France?"

Ewa shook her head, her golden curls dancing in the warm lighting of the dining car. "America. I went there for college shortly after my parents passed." She lifted her cup, sipped, left just the smallest trace of scarlet lipstick along the edge. "My brother's idea to go there."

"Which school?" Frost asked, taking a drink of his own coffee, surprised at how easy it was to talk to this woman. There was something about her, he thought. Something comfortable. Something that, after those first few panicked moments, felt very easy and fitting and kind.

"Princeton, at first," she was saying. "Then Chicago."

"The sciences?" Frost guessed. "Mathematics?"

"Heavens, no," she laughed. "I mean, I can do those things—chemistry and physics and calculus—but I don't like them." Another sip. A warm smile. "I chose something I liked."

"And what was that?"

"Literature," she answered.

"Really?" Frost said. "English? German?"

"All kinds," she said. "Anything I could get my hands on." She finished her coffee, lifted the linen napkin and dabbed at the corners of her mouth, her mannerisms smooth and economical and somehow amazingly feminine.

"Any favorites? Among my fellow Americans, I mean?"

A sheepish grin began creeping across her face. "Plenty, though I've been told that liking certain genres of literature is not proper for a woman."

Frost cocked his head and let an eyebrow rise below the curled flop of hair falling across his brow.

"Horror," she said, flushing. "I find your Mr. Poe so delightfully morbid." She looked thoroughly embarrassed by the admission. "It's horrible, isn't it? To be so very fascinated by his writing."

Frost let a gentle smile creep across his own face. "Not at all. I enjoyed my share of Shelley and Stoker when I was in school. I'm certain my parents disapproved of them." He shrugged. "My mother especially. She never understood why I liked reading things like that."

Ewa nodded, her eyes wide and soft and bright. "Mine either. And I know what they would say if they were still alive." She lowered her voice several octaves, assuming a mocking tone that Frost found charming. She waggled a finger. "It's just not ladylike, Ewa, to read such things. Stick to the classics, young lady. To proper literature."

She laughed.

A wild and insane feeling raced through Frost's mind, through his veins. He tried to tell himself that it was nothing. That the feeling was crazy. But…

He loved the laugh. Her laugh. Loved how it fell into his ears and penetrated his soul. It was warm and jovial and genuine. Light as crystal and bright as the noon sun.

"I have no idea what they meant by that. Proper literature," she continued. "Rabelais? Dickens? Dumas? Homer?" She paused. "If I'm honest, I am certain my brother thinks as they do. Advocates for the old stuff. Refuses to acknowledge anything new."

"Would they consider Poe new?" Frost asked. Jesus, he thought. The man's been dead for what? Ninety years?

"I'm sure that they would consider anything less than one hundred years old new," she answered, "but if you really want to know, you can ask him yourself." She looked over Frost's shoulder.

Frost turned, looking back toward the door to the dining car where two men had just entered and were speaking to the maître d'.

The first man, the younger of the two, was trim and fit-looking. He wore a well-fitted gray suit, a stiff pinstriped shirt, and a maroon silk necktie. He sported a faint tan on his face and hands, and had short, neatly-trimmed blond hair and sharp, piercing blue eyes.

That must be her brother, Frost thought, still watching as the man pointed to the corner of the car where Frost sat and began heading that way with his companion in tow.

The companion was older, Frost saw. He wore an impeccably tailored suit—black with thin, white pinstripes—over a pair of the most highly polished shoes Frost had ever seen. The shirt was blazingly white and stiff, and the necktie knotted in place at the top of the collar was a brilliant goldenrod paisley silk. His hair was dark, nearly black, with the faintest wisps of gray just beginning to show. He had a wide forehead, heavy brows, and dark eyes whose color Frost could not make out. Small clusters of wrinkles were starting to gather at the corners of the eyes, Frost saw, and the man's cheeks were just beginning to sag. Not jowls. Not quite yet. But getting there.

Frost stood as the men approached. Ewa joined him.

"Elias," she said. "This is Ridge Frost, from America."

Frost stuck his hand out and the younger man took it, the grip youthful and strong and confident. He did not see the faint cloud pass over Ewa's face.

"A pleasure," Frost said.

"The pleasure is all mine," said Fischer. He turned to the man with him. "Ewa, Herr Frost, may I introduce Sir Gerald Thornhill?"

The older man's hand came out, a tired smile working its way across his face. "Call me Gerry, please. All my friends do."

The accent, Frost noted was pure, educated, English. It reminded him of the Royal Marine officers he'd had contact with in Shanghai. Eton, he thought. Eton and then Oxford and then…

Frost took Thornhill's hand, shook it. "Ridge, please." He turned to the table, waved at it with his free hand. "I was just finishing up. The table is yours if you like."

Thornhill released the handshake. Fischer laughed, smiled. "Nonsense," he said. "This is your table and it would be completely improper of us to chase you away from it. We would join you, though, if that is acceptable?"

"I'd be delighted," Frost said.

The group arranged themselves at the small table, Frost next to Thornhill and Ewa next to her brother.

"Bit of a tight fit, isn't it?" Thornhill noted, easing himself into his seat. "I'm afraid these old knees aren't quite as supple as they used to be."

"I've been in tighter places," Frost allowed, edging sideways to give the older man a little extra space.

"How's that?" Thornhill asked.

"Ridge was a Marine," Ewa said. Frost looked at her, saw that she was as far away from Elias as she could get on the small seat. He also noted that she did not look at her brother. Her eyes, which had been lively and bright, had changed somehow. There was something there that Frost did not like. A hunted and cowed look that was…

Curious.

Thornhill's face came around and Fischer's head came up.

"Really? An American *and* a Marine?" Thornhill said. "Been anywhere exciting?"

"I was with the Fourth Marines in Shanghai a few years ago. Was there during Soochow Creek."

Thornhill had turned away from Frost to accept a menu from their waiter. Frost did not see the dark cloud flit across the man's face. He did notice Fischer's eyebrow twitch up.

"And since then?" Thornhill asked, turning back from the waiter.

Frost paused before answering. He glanced at Ewa, saw her try to force a smile, and wondered what had changed. Then, he heard Henry Jackson's voice in his head, telling him that his backstory *was* the backstory. The cover. A disgruntled Marine. An angry American. Looking for a fresh start. Why not Berlin?

"The brig," Frost admitted, hoping that the truth would explain away the brief pause, watching everyone at the table for reactions.

He saw Ewa wince, look down at her lap, and begin to blush, the color in her pale cheeks rising quickly. Thornhill and Fischer were both looking at him now. Thornhill's face held an expression that was part curiosity and part mystery. There was something there that Frost couldn't place. Fischer kept his face mostly neutral, allowing only his eyebrows to rise, the question there obvious.

He wants to know the story, Frost thought. Wants me to tell it, but he's too polite to ask.

Frost smiled at Fischer and shrugged his shoulders. "I had a run-in with my brigadier, my commander," Frost explained. "Things went badly, I blamed him, and I hit him in the face. I got two years in the brig for that. Got out last week and decided to jump ship, as it were."

Fischer nodded, looked down at his menu. "And now you're here, on a train to Berlin."

It was a question. Frost understood that. He shrugged again, hoping that the gesture translated well. Ewa, he saw, still looked a little embarrassed. And something else. What?

"Why not, I figured. My family is mostly German. Emigrated from Dortmund about four generations back." Frost smiled at Fischer. "And frankly, there isn't much honest work available back home for someone who just got kicked out of the service the way I did."

Fischer smiled back, a thin, knowing smile. He turned to look at Ewa. "And you two met in America?" he said, turning back to Frost. "Is that how you know each other?"

Frost shook his head. "Actually, no. We just met. I was in here getting ready to order and the maître d' asked if I would be willing to share my table with a young lady."

Frost saw Ewa's face change. She lifted her eyes to him. A gentle, almost imperceptible smile began to form. It vanished quickly, before anyone else could see it.

"Ridge was kind enough to offer me a seat at his table," she said to her brother. Again, without looking at him. "Elias is a military man, by the way. He's a, what's the word for it? A captain? Is that right?"

Fischer began to respond, but the waiter appeared at his elbow. He and Thornhill ordered their meals and sent the waiter on his way.

"Actually," Thornhill said to Ewa, "your brother has been promoted. And given a new assignment."

Ewa winced. Frost saw it. He was certain, however, that no one else noticed. What in the hell?

"Really? When did this happen?" she asked.

"Right before you got on the plane from America to Paris," Fischer said. "It's why I am returning to Berlin with you."

"And?" Ewa asked.

"And what?" Fischer said.

"What's the promotion?"

Fischer shrugged, toying with his water glass.

"What he's too modest to admit, dear Ewa, is that he is now Oberführer Fischer, Commandant of Sachsenhausen."

Frost saw a pained expression cloud Ewa's face for a brief moment. Then it vanished. "Oberführer," he said. "That's a colonel, correct?"

"Yes," Fischer said. "The positions are roughly similar."

"Congratulations," Frost offered.

Fischer inclined his head, smiled, and reached into an inside pocket of his suit. He withdrew a small golden case, three inches by five inches square. He also withdrew a compact golden lighter, simple and plain and rectangular in shape, the gleaming surface marred only by a thin swastika etched on each of the object's widest surfaces. He opened the case, selected a cigarette, placed it between his lips, and lit it before offering the case to Frost and Thornhill.

Frost declined with a polite wave of his hand, as did Thornhill. Fischer shrugged and laid the case and lighter flat on the table.

"Mother hated that, Elias," Ewa said without looking away from the table. "You know that."

Fischer looked amused at the remark. He sucked on the gold-tipped cigarette, held his breath, and then exhaled a thin, wispy cloud of sweet, blue smoke. He ignored his sister and addressed Frost.

"So, Herr Frost, what are your plans when we get to Berlin?"

Frost offered a gallic shrug. "Try to find work, I suppose. Something honest."

"Not interested in joining the Wehrmacht?" Thornhill asked.

"I'd prefer to put my education to work, if at all possible, but…" Frost let his voice trail off as if to imply that he wouldn't be opposed to joining the German Army if it came to that.

"Are you a literary man?" Fischer asked. "Like my darling sister, here?"

Frost shook his head, decided to lie. Admitting to having a degree in physics was, he judged, a little too truthful, but…

"Engineering," Frost said.

"Ah." Fischer grinned. "Engineering. A man's job. The Fatherland can always find suitable employment for a good engineer. I daresay that, were you so inclined, the military could find many uses for you. Apart from carrying a rifle or driving a tank." He pointed the half-smoked cigarette at Frost, waggling the orange tip. "Research and development. They are always in search of good, intelligent, loyal people. Men who can think and solve. To design the next battle tank or fighter."

"I'd be happy to help. After the last two years," Frost said, "I just want to keep my head down and earn my keep."

Thornhill clapped him on the shoulder, laughing. "Spoken like a true socialist. You'll fit right in with this lot."

Frost grinned at the older man. "I've got to ask. You're obviously British. Living in Berlin?"

"Guilty as charged," Thornhill said.

"What do you do?"

"A little of this. Some of that," Thornhill offered. "Like you just said. Happy to help where I can."

Fischer stubbed out his finished cigarette and lit another. He smiled, shaking his head. "What Herr Thornhill is too polite to tell you, Frost, is that he is almost single-handedly rebuilding the German banking system."

"Reforming," Thornhill chided. "Not rebuilding. Just some minor adjustments here and there. Advice."

Fischer ignored Thornhill. "Rebuilding. Why, just last month, he had several meetings with the Führer himself. Just the two of them."

"Hitler?" Frost asked, turning to Thornhill. "Really?"

"In the flesh," Fischer said.

"I just answered a few questions the man had, that's all," Thornhill said. "My dear Elias, you really make too much of my meager assistance."

"Bah. Nonsense," Fischer said. He turned back to Frost. "He really is too modest. Why, if it weren't for him and his efforts, the economists in my country would still be trading pelts for goods and services."

Thornhill offered his own, embarrassed shrug.

The waiter arrived, bearing several plates of food for Thornhill and Fischer.

Frost used the opportunity to excuse himself, thanking everyone for the conversation and agreeing to meet the group later in the bar car for drinks.

———

The man from Paris checked his watch when the target left the dining car, calculating the time until the train's next stop.

"Our guy made some new friends," he said. "Who do you suppose they are?"

"Planned contacts?" asked the second man.

The man from Paris thought for a moment and shook his head. "Possible, but I don't think so."

"Germans?"

The man from Paris stood, reached into his pocket, and dropped money on the table to cover his meal and drinks. "The blond man and woman, yes. I think so. But the older man…" He shrugged. "I'm heading forward to wake Albrecht. He can keep watch while I get some sleep."

The second man nodded, pretended to be interested in his newspaper. "Suit yourself. I'll be here."

9 | A Change of Plans

Two hours later, with the table cleared of their dishes and with small cups of fresh coffee in front of them, Fischer and Thornhill both rose when Ewa announced her intent to return to her cabin. Both men bowed in that short and rather stiff manner peculiar to Nazi Germany: a short click of the heels against each other and a small, rigid inclination of the head. Under these circumstances, the standard salutes were replaced with warm smiles as Ewa curtsied and left the dining car.

Both men resumed their seats.

"And I half expected you to kneel and kiss her hand," Fischer teased. He withdrew another cigarette, tapped it against the case, and lit it. He looked at his companion's face, expecting to see amusement there. But what he saw was… what? "Something on your mind, Herr Thornhill?"

"This man, Frost," Thornhill began, his voice hovering and slow. "What do you know of him?"

A shrug. "Nothing more than you. Why?"

Thornhill turned, looked to the dining car's exit, speaking almost to himself. "I don't know. Something about him. Something… I don't know. Familiar?" He turned back to Fischer. "Almost as if I've met him before."

"Have you?" Fischer asked. "Met him before, I mean?"

Thornhill wrinkled his brow, ignoring the question. "It's that thing he said, about his time with the Fourth Marines." Thornhill paused, thinking hard. "There were Marines involved in the warehouse raid. The one I told you about. Resh sent me there to help persuade some Chinese banker. I don't remember his name."

Fischer looked up, puzzled. "You've lost me."

Thornhill explained for several minutes, occasionally pausing to look over his shoulder at the car's door.

"It's the damnedest thing," he said. "I cannot get clear of the feeling that I have seen that man before. But…"

Fischer leaned back in his seat, pulling at the cigarette and exhaling thin clouds of wispy blue smoke. "Well, it's no matter." He glanced at his watch and smiled sleepily. "We'll be in Berlin in twelve hours. I'll need to report the contact to Kapitan Hanssen at OKW at the next stop. I'll do that, and someone will look into the man, and that will be that." Another pull at the cigarette. Another long, luxurious exhalation. "I expect that he's just what he says he is. An ex-Marine. Disgruntled with America. Looking to start over somewhere. He wouldn't be the first." He smiled maliciously at Thornhill. "Sounds rather like you in that way."

Thornhill missed the barb. He was turned, looking at the door and thinking.

———

The train made its first stop inside the German border thirty minutes later. The man from Paris rose, grateful for the short rest, left the train, and made another call. After relaying his most recent report—mostly that the subject had done nothing but sleep—he was told to hang up and to call back in ten minutes. He waited, watching the crowds and glancing at his watch. Precisely ten minutes later, he was on the phone again. He spoke. He listened carefully. He repeated the new orders when he was directed to do so.

"Do you understand?"

The man said he did.

"Good." The line went dead.

The man from Paris swiped at the perspiration on his brow and wondered what had changed. He left the booth and headed back to his train. On the way, he bumped into two men. He apologized and kept heading for the platform without noticing that the two men were his target's dining companions.

———

Frost walked into the train's bar car an hour after the train began rolling again. Ewa, he saw, was already there. He smiled at her, waved, and moved to a seat at her table. From somewhere unseen, music wafted through the car. Marlene Dietrich's 'Naughty Lola,' Frost realized. A waiter appeared at his elbow.

"A drink, monsieur?"

"Bourbon," he said. "Two fingers. Neat."

"Very good, monsieur." The waiter turned. "And you, mademoiselle? A second wine, perhaps?"

Ewa shook her head and pointed to the half-full glass in front of her.

The waiter left.

"Am I late?" Frost made a show of checking his watch.

Ewa laughed. "Not at all. I was thirsty and bored." She shrugged. "So, I came early."

Frost smiled. The waiter brought his drink, set it on the table, bowed, and departed. Frost lifted the drink, swirled it in the tumbler. He could smell it. The thick, syrupy-sweet notes of caramel and vanilla and the rough, faint scent of charred oak. He sipped the drink, felt it trace its heated path across his tongue and down the back of his throat. He looked at Ewa, saw her face change. Saw the smile disappear. Replaced with…

"What is it?" he asked.

"Let me guess," said the voice of Elias Fischer. "Bourbon. Not scotch?"

Frost put his drink down on the table. He turned to look at the newcomers. "Call it a preference," he said. "From my upbringing."

Fischer and Thornhill took seats at the small, rounded table. The waiter was there immediately to take their orders.

"I believe that a good beer is in order," Fischer pronounced. "Something thick and dark." He reviewed the menu and made his selection.

"Very good, monsieur," the waiter said, and turned to Thornhill. "Et vous?"

"What kind of sherry do you have?"

The waiter listed three, briefly describing the finer points of each. Thornhill selected one. The waiter nodded his approval, departed, and was back in less than a minute with the order.

Two cars forward, the man from Paris was cursing. He wasn't equipped for this type of thing. Neither were the additional men. They were strictly watchers. That's what they'd been trained to do. They sat and walked and observed and reported. They made notes. Wrote down times and places and names, if they discovered them. They were not murderers.

Not that this was murder, he reminded himself. It couldn't be. The target had been identified as a spy. Kapitan Hanssen had said so. The target had been sent from America to steal secrets. It did not matter which secrets. It did not matter how Kapitan Hanssen had come across the information, though the man from Paris did speculate. Someone close to the target. In the same building or office? Likely.

And irrelevant. The man was a spy. And spies were to be put to death upon discovery. By the Führer's orders.

But they were supposed to be put to death by people trained to do these things. People who were equipped for this sort of thing. With pistols or rifles or bombs or whatever.

He had a knife. Not even a good one. Not something you'd use to kill a man. A small, folding knife. The kind his grandfather had once used to whittle down sticks into nothing but a pile of shavings and toothpicks.

But it's what he had. All he had.

And he was the only one armed.

"*Die Arschmade*," he hissed to himself. Son of a bitch. He pulled the knife from a pocket, shoved the blade open with his thumb, the movement economical and efficient. He fingered the blade and forced himself to think.

———

"So, Herr Frost." Fischer grinned and hefted his second beer of the evening. "Dare I ask about whatever happened in Shanghai? Did you really hit your commanding general?"

Frost nodded and sipped at his drink, enjoying the slow, smooth burn of the liquor. The music had changed. Fred Astaire now. 'Cheek to Cheek.' "I did. Broke his nose."

"Why?"

Frost looked at his companions. Fischer was clearly interested in him. He was leaning forward, eager and ready to listen. Thornhill, by contrast, was trying his best to stay impassive. He had a look on his face that Frost took to be displeasure, as if the incident in question was somehow improper.

Or he thinks I'm uncouth, Frost thought. A barbarian.

"Elias," Ewa protested. "You shouldn't pester him about such things."

Fischer waved a dismissive hand at her. "Nonsense." He swallowed a large draught of his dark beer and turned to Frost. "She wouldn't understand, Herr Frost. She's never served in the military. Neither has Gerry. But us? Men like us understand. What you did, what you claim to have done, is something we all fantasize about. Especially when one is kept under the boot heel of a buffoon." Fischer took another big gulp of his beer and set the mug down. "So, tell me, what happened in Shanghai?"

Frost relayed the story over a fifteen-minute period, watching the faces of his audience. Ewa's face showed nothing but sorrow at the story, a profound sadness that Frost found hard to look at. Fischer smiled for the duration, especially when Frost described the shelling of the bridge and the last confrontation with the general.

And Thornhill?

His face had changed slightly during the telling, right when Frost had been describing the assault on the warehouse. There was something there Frost couldn't place. An emotion that didn't quite fit the mood. Like he's chewing over something in his head, Frost thought.

But what?

"I am so sorry," Ewa said. "How did your mother handle it? Randolph killed and you off to the brig."

Frost only barely avoided wincing at the question. He was saved from answering when Fischer cut in.

"But how did it feel? When your fist smashed into the general's face?"

Frost watched the man's face, saw that he was enjoying the story. Maybe a little too much? Frost thought that over, wondered about it. Was the enjoyment feigned or real? If it was feigned, what did that say about the man? That he was acting? For Frost's benefit? And if the excessive enjoyment was real? Well, then, that would make Fischer something of a sociopathic personality. Or psychopathic?

Frost couldn't remember which was which. He let his eyes drift to Ewa's face, saw the pain there. Saw the way her eyes twitched nervously to the side. To her left. To where Elias was sitting.

She's scared of him, his mind reported. No. Not scared. Terrified. A fleeting thought drifting into Frost's head. He'd seen this kind of behavior before. His own mother. The demure way she'd answered his father's questions. The way she wouldn't make eye contact. How she tried to hide the flinches whenever his hands began moving or when his voice had that sharp edge to it. That bite.

Dad, Frost thought, used to beat Mom. Used to beat the shit out of her.

He eyed Ewa and Elias, decided that he probably wasn't beating her. But damned if she isn't scared of him.

Frost was not surprised to feel his pulse quickening at the thought. He found that he had developed a nearly insatiable urge to reach out and slam Fischer's head into the table.

"Honestly," he answered, "I thought about that while I was in the brig, and the only thing I've been able to decide is that I was too angry to feel anything but the anger." He paused. "I just had this rage inside me, and I hit him and felt everything melt away with the punch."

Fischer sipped his beer and seemed to take the thought under consideration. "Would you do it again?"

Frost had spent nearly two full years in the brig asking himself that very question. And the honest answer was…

"I don't know." He shrugged. "I know that's not an exciting answer, but it's the best I've got."

Ewa was nodding, Frost noticed. Fischer lifted his beer and held it up to Frost, a queer smile forcing the left side of his mouth up at the corner. "Well, the past is the past, and now you're here. In a few hours, you'll be in Berlin, and, civilian or not, the Führer will find a purpose for you."

Frost lifted his own glass with a sideways glance at both Ewa and Thornhill. Ewa looked nervous. Thornhill looked confused. Fischer downed the remnants of his beer, called for another round, and leaned forward with both elbows on the tabletop.

"Now, Herr Frost, for the important part of our little discussion." He let his grin widen considerably. "I need your help with something."

Frost looked at the man, felt his pulse race. He lifted his glass, took a small sip. Swallowed. "What's that?"

The grin got even bigger. "I need you to explain the devilry that is American football."

———

Two hours later, the man from Paris watched as the target walked down the center aisle of the train car. He'd been waiting for the man to head back to his own car. Had watched him drink and talk. Had watched him dance with the pretty blonde. Had even tagged along as the man walked the young lady back to her cabin. He'd seen the light kiss she'd bestowed on the target and had felt a brief flicker of shame about what he planned to do.

He waited until the target passed through the doors at the opposite end of the car before he rose to follow. His left hand swung free, the right slipping into his pants pocket and closing around the handle of the small knife, hoping that it was large enough to do the job. He'd read about doing this, the science and technique of the thing, only once, and his brain worked to recall the information as he passed through to the next car, his eyes wandering left and right without ever fully leaving the target's back.

Hand on the face, he told himself. Slip the knife in right above the collar. Easier said than done, he thought.

The target passed on to the next car and the man from Paris followed.

Two more cars, the man thought. Catch him right outside his room. Let him unlock the door. Slip the knife in. And hide him in his own cabin.

He passed through another set of doors. One more car, he thought. His body started to tense. The hand in his pocket gripped the knife tight enough to cause the muscles to ache from his wrist to his elbow.

The target passed through the last set of doors. The man from Paris walked faster, the hand clutching the knife starting to come out of his pocket. His left hand reached for the door. His heart raced. Sweat formed and fell. Across his brow. Along his spine, the tracks it traced hot at first, but cooling rapidly. The hairs on his neck stood on end. He could see the target just through the doors, nearly to his cabin. The man from Paris felt his left hand seize the handle of the inter-car doors.

"Halt."

The voice came from the man's right, a softy spoken but hard command. He spun around, looking for the source of the voice. The cabin door on his right was open. A man was sitting inside the cabin, with his legs crossed and a newspaper in his hands. Above the paper, a set of impossibly blue eyes were staring at him. The paper lowered. The face smiled at him.

"Let me guess," said the face. "You are one of the watchers from OKW, yes?"

The man from Paris was too stunned to answer. He looked left, through the doors, saw the target's cabin door closing.

"Ignore him," said the man with the paper. "Answer my question. You work for Kapitan Hanssen, yes?"

"Who the hell are you?" the man from Paris growled.

The man with the paper cocked his head to one side, folded his paper, and stood. He reached inside his suit coat, withdrew a small leather folder, and held it open. "I am Oberführer Fischer. Commandant of Sachsenhausen." Fischer let the words hang in the air, waited for recognition to dawn on the man in front of him. When the eyes finally went slightly wide and the shoulders twitched, he went on. "I understand what your orders were." He emphasized the last word. "I am countermanding your orders. You will leave this man to me. Understand?"

"But he is a spy," the man from Paris stammered. "He is a spy and…"

"And," Fischer said, "it is much smarter to follow such people." A short pause. "Think. If he is, as you say, a spy, then he is being sent here to go somewhere or meet someone. Yes?"

The man from Paris nodded uneasily.

"And wouldn't it be nice to know who he is meeting or where he is looking?"

Another nod.

"So, you will leave him to me," Fischer repeated.

"But Kapitan Hanssen…"

"If the good Kapitan needs to know who prevented you from following your orders, you will give him my name and position. Tell him I threatened you."

"But you did not threaten me," said the man from Paris.

Fischer reached to unbutton his suit coat. "Do you need me to?"

The man shook his head violently.

"And you will leave your target to me?"

A violent nod.

"Good." Fischer held a hand out. "Now give me the knife in your pocket and go enjoy the rest of the trip. There is a tab in the bar car with my name on it. Get a drink. Get your men drinks."

The man hesitated for a single moment before handing over the knife and heading back the way he'd come.

Fischer dropped the knife in the trash, knocked on the door to the small lavatory, and resumed his seat. He lifted the paper.

The door to the lavatory opened. Thornhill poked his head out. "How did you know?"

"Hanssen told me."

"When?"

Fischer looked up from his paper, smiled. "At the last stop, when we went out to the phones at the station. We actually bumped into that man, remember?"

Thornhill moved out of the lavatory, shut the door, and leaned against it. "What does Hanssen know?"

"Not much. Enough, though. What he's after. His name. Some background. His contact's information."

"What's he after?"

Fischer turned the page. He did not look up. "Uranverein."

"Bloody hell," Thornhill breathed. "Who's the contact?"

Fischer told him. "They call him Locksmith."

Thornhill came off the door. "Fucking hell, Elias. Do you think…"

Fischer turned another page of his paper. "I don't." He paused, read something, laughed, and looked to Thornhill. He saw how agitated the man was. "Relax, Gerry. He's not after you or me or Resh. He's after the atomic weapons research. That's it."

"You're quite sure," Thornhill hissed.

Fischer shrugged. "Hanssen is. Says his source is impeccable. Says he has heard recordings of the briefings this man Frost got before he left and some conversations earlier today. No mention of Resh or VEIL. Just Hitler and his bomb project." Fischer returned to his paper. "Nonsense, if you ask me. The bomb project. And completely unnecessary." Another page turn. Another pause to read. Another chuckle. "The invasion will kick off on September first, and we'll waltz our way across Europe and have ourselves a grand time." He folded the paper and tossed it aside. "And when it's all over, Resh will have backed the winning side. He'll have the whole damned world eating out of his hands. Think of it, Gerry. Just think. One massive organization controlling everything. Economies. War. Peace. With the power to appoint those willing to serve him and cast aside those who stand in his way."

Thornhill said nothing.

"With Resh's blessing, you could return to Britain, Gerry. Not as a citizen or a subject, but as a king. You could do that, if you keep your head. And I, Gerry," Fischer offered a thin, dangerous smile, "I could supplant the Führer himself."

10 | Arrivés à Berlin

"Mesdames et messieurs, nous sommes arrivés à Berlin." The voice was bright and clear, and the words were repeated, in German, with a small variance. Welcome to Berlin, Frost's mind translated as he stepped from the train to the platform at Anhalter Bahnhof. He checked his watch, saw that it was five minutes past ten in the morning. His contact would not be here, so he didn't bother looking for a person. What he did look for were signs. Something leading the way out of the massive, gothic building. Something that would lead out into the day and, maybe, hopefully, to a row of waiting taxicabs.

"Do you need a ride, Herr Frost?"

Frost turned to see Ewa, Fischer, and Thornhill behind him. All three appeared to be freshly scrubbed and were immaculately dressed in clean, pressed clothes. Thornhill was wearing a light gray suit, pinstriped in burgundy, with a light blue shirt and dark, cross-hatched tie. Fischer, Frost saw, wore the stiff, black uniform of an SS Oberführer. Thick silver braids adorned each of his shoulders, and twin, elegantly embroidered laurels graced the point of each collar. On his left arm, just above the elbow, flashed a bright red band with a swastika ensconced in a white circle. His right breast was adorned with an array of medals, and, at his throat, Frost saw a thick band of ribbon and an Iron Cross.

Wonder what he got that for, Frost thought.

His mind, and his body, stopped cold when he saw Ewa. She wore a little ebony-black viscose dress, with gathered shoulders and a plunging, cross-over neckline that was simultaneously demure and alluring. The dress hugged her small waist and flared as it fell, floating with her as she walked. On her feet she wore a pair of black-and-cream patent-leather spectator pumps. Her thick, solid heels clicked on the polished marble of the train station floor. Her face was lightly made up: a little rouge, some faint traces of eyeshadow, and a brilliant, wine-colored lipstick that was perfectly applied.

Frost felt his heart skip a beat, felt his stomach flutter. He smiled at her. She smiled back. Fischer, looking at the both of them, also smiled. He held a hand out. Frost took it.

"We have a car, Herr Frost," he said. "We can drop you off on the way."

Frost looked around the station, watched the mass of travelers rushing to and fro, heard the cacophony of voices, most featuring the rapid, edgy intonation common to German. He looked at Thornhill, saw the impassive face. He turned to Fischer.

"That would be fine," he said. "I'd appreciate that."

A porter stopped to collect the group's baggage, and, with Fischer's directions, they were off, weaving through the various kiosks and stands dotting the concourse.

The group exited through the massive array of doors and into the gray overcast of a late-summer day. A soft drizzle assaulted them, falling almost like a mist from a thin, cloudy sky. The temperature, Frost judged, could not have been much more than sixty, the air made chilly by the swirling water vapor and light breeze.

"Here we are," Fischer said, his voice as jovial and as light as the station announcer's had been. He led the way down a short set of stairs to the street where a jet-black Mercedes sedan sat against the curb.

Frost was admiring the car when Fischer's hand fell on his shoulder.

"What hotel, Herr Frost?"

Frost had to think for a moment, his eyes tracing the cabriolet's gentle curves and noting the twin flags affixed to the vehicle's front fender wells.

"Hotel Kaiserhof," Frost said. "I hope it isn't too far out of your way."

"An excellent choice, Mr. Frost," Thornhill said, hefting his bag and Ewa's into the Mercedes' trunk. "I stayed there for my first month in Berlin." He turned to Fischer. "What was it? A year ago?"

Fischer hefted his own bags into the vehicle's trunk. "I believe so." He shifted his gaze, reached for Frost's luggage. "Allow me."

"You're sure this isn't out of the way?" Frost asked again.

"Not at all." Fischer placed Frost's bags in the trunk and closed the lid. "We are heading for the Reich Chancellery, and your hotel is just across the street." He paused, surveyed his surroundings, lifted his face to the sky. "It is good to be home. Paris is lovely, but…"

"Can we get in the car?" Ewa asked. "Please?"

Everyone turned to Ewa. Her blonde locks were collecting the gentle rain quickly, and they were already hanging limp and lank along the sides of her face.

"Of course," Fischer said, his voice still light. "Of course. My apologies." He reached for the nearest door of the car, a rear one, unlocked and opened it, gallantly extending an arm. "Ewa. Herr Frost. If you will…"

Frost followed Ewa into the car's lush rear seat and the door was shut behind them. Fischer crawled into the front passenger seat, and Thornhill, Frost was surprised to see, climbed behind the steering wheel.

"You aren't driving?" Ewa asked her brother.

He turned, smiling. "No. Gerry spent most of our time in Paris badgering me about my driving. I figure it is time to give in."

Thornhill started the car and Frost felt the low, powerful rumble of the six cylinders vibrate through the car.

"I'll try to stay on the correct side of the roadway," Thornhill joked. He looked into the rearview mirror and offered Frost a wink before turning the wheel and racing away from the curb.

Ten minutes later, Thornhill angled the big car out of traffic and guided it to the curb in front of the Hotel Kaiserhof. He watched in the mirror as Frost and Ewa exited the vehicle, elbowing Fischer as Frost pulled his bags from the trunk and set them on the sidewalk.

"I think your sister fancies the Yank."

Fischer looked up, turned in his seat to look out the rear window, peering through the rivulets of precipitation that collected together and traveled down the smooth, flat glass. The smile on his face faltered slightly. Frost and Ewa were standing in the drizzle, not much more than arm's length away from each other. Their hands came together briefly in what appeared simply to be a friendly handshake, both of her hands clasping one of his.

Except…

"What was that?" Fischer asked. He turned to Thornhill. "You saw that. Tell me you saw that."

Thornhill grunted. He'd seen it. In the brief moment when Ewa's hands and Frost's hands had parted, he'd seen it. A flash of white where none should have been. "She passed him a note. Wonder what it said."

Fischer swore.

Thornhill turned to him. "What?"

"I shouldn't have told her."

Thornhill cocked his head. "Told her what, old boy?"

"That Herr Frost is under suspicion. That OKW believes he is a spy."

"Have you lost your mind? Why would you tell her that?" Thornhill felt his pulse race. His mind began working. Trying to recall. Again. A series of images danced in front of his eyes. He struggled again to place Frost, convinced he'd seen the face before somewhere. Shanghai, his mind told him. It had to be Shanghai. He thought about the fight in the warehouse. About the Marines blowing the doors in. The smoke. The gunfire. And then, when it was all over, when he'd been pulled upright…

Damn. Had that been Frost? His unit? Was it possible that Frost was here for him? For Resh? For VEIL? He pondered the question. It was possible. Possible, but unlikely. There was simply no way the Americans could know about his organization. Hell, he thought, the Nazis and Japanese hadn't known about it until they'd been approached. No, that wasn't true. The Nazis and Japanese still did not know. Not as a whole. Just a few select individuals. The men with their hands on the strings. Hitler. Himmler. And that skinny bastard, Goebbels. Tojo. Suzuki. Konoe. And Hirota.

He shook his head to clear it, refocused on the problem at hand. "Why in the bloody hell would you tell her that?"

Fischer ignored the question, turned back to the front of the car, his brow furrowed and his lips pursed. "Maybe," he muttered. "Yes."

"Yes what?" Thornhill asked. He could feel the anger rising, bubbling up. "Yes what, Elias?"

But Fischer was already out of the car. Thornhill followed suit, popping open the driver's side door and stepping back into the cold drizzle.

"Everything alright?" Fischer asked Frost.

"Yes," Frost said, his hands disappearing into his pockets. "I was just asking Ewa here if she might be interested in dinner tonight."

Thornhill watched Fischer's face light up. "A brilliant idea, Herr Frost," he said. "The both of you should have dinner. And afterwards, as it happens, there is an event tonight that I meant to invite you to. You and Ewa both. At the Sports Palace."

Ewa, Thornhill saw, looked wary.

Frost's face cracked into a wide smile. "I'd be delighted, Elias," he said. "What time?"

Fischer provided the details and took the liberty of suggesting a restaurant.

"Will you be joining us for dinner?" Frost asked.

Fischer smiled warmly and flashed his eyes toward Ewa. "I think, Herr Frost, that my sister would prefer that I did not."

"You have no objection to our having dinner?"

A laugh. "Not at all, sir. I wish my sister to be happy, and you seem like a gentleman." He clapped his hands together. "I could not be more pleased." He looked at his watch. "Now, if you'll excuse us, I must get Ewa home. Herr Thornhill and I have business to attend to."

Thornhill watched as Fischer shook hands with Frost and escorted his sister back to the car. He nodded at Frost, glanced at the bags and the hotel's entrance, forced a smile. "You had better get inside, Mr. Frost, before this bloody weather gets any worse."

He watched Frost collect his bags and disappear into the hotel before climbing back behind the wheel of the big Mercedes and driving away.

Frost, carrying his own bags, entered suite 707 of the Hotel Kaiserhof fifteen minutes later to find a small, shaggy-haired man waiting in his sitting room.

"I figured you'd be lurking in the lobby somewhere, waiting for me to get here." Frost tried to not sound annoyed. He was here to collect a single file from a contact called Locksmith, and, despite what had happened at the Mayflower, he thought the whole thing too fictional. Too cloak-and-dagger. Too dramatic. Like something out of a book. Mysterious and crafty for the sake of being mysterious and crafty. It was, he judged, all being overdone.

"I'm Lyle," said the shaggy man, not bothering to stand. His accent was pure Bronx, but with something else that Frost couldn't quite place. Something almost southern. "How was the trip?"

Frost set his bags down, then straightened and stretched. "Not bad. Long. Would have preferred to take a ship across."

"Henry told me you didn't particularly enjoy flying," the man said. He fished a pack of cigarettes and a book of matches out of a pocket and held them up. When Frost shook his head, the man shrugged, lit a cigarette, exhaled contentedly, and continued. "Anyways, who's the broad?"

Frost bristled at the comment, eyed the man, saw the grin, and bit off his first response. He wondered at his reaction. He wasn't falling for her, was he? He smiled at the absurdity of the thought and then noted that it might not be absurd at all. She had asked him to dinner, despite what he'd said to Fischer. And she'd kissed him goodnight the previous evening, when they'd all finished their drinks and he'd walked her back to her cabin on the train. "Someone I met on the train. Brother is an SS man." Frost paused. "Oberführer Fischer. Commandant of a place called Sachsenhausen. Heard of it?"

Lyle inhaled and sent smoke swirling around above his head. "Only rumors. Work camp. A prison, really. A bit like the chain gang stuff we have back home, only these folks stay inside the wire." He shrugged. "*Alles in Ordnung*, as they say here."

Frost hefted one of his bags onto the dresser and opened it. "So, when do I meet this contact?"

"Tonight, if you like, though I might need more time to make the arrangements. He's a busy kind of guy. Right up there in the top row of Nazis with the mustachioed poobah himself."

Frost began transferring the contents of the suitcase to one of the dresser drawers.

Lyle shifted in his seat, crossed one leg over the other, and let his foot dangle comfortably. "On second thought, tonight might be too soon. Your man is supposed to be at a speech tonight. At the Sports Palace. Hitler is the main event, and the whole thing is by invitation only."

Frost held up two shirts, considered them, and put both in the drawer, opting for a third shirt that was plain white. He carried his selection into the bathroom with the rest of the articles of clothing he'd selected for the night and hung them up on the back of the door. "In that case," Frost said, walking back into the sitting room, "there's no problem meeting our man tonight."

"Maybe you didn't hear me right, sport," Lyle admonished gently. "I need to get you an invitation first. Without one, you can't get into the speech, and without getting in, you can't make contact with our man."

Frost smiled at Lyle. "I have an invitation," he said. He outlined the dinner plans and invitation.

"So, this SS man invited you to see the Führer speak? Just like that? Out of the blue?" Lyle sounded worried.

"Yeah," Frost said. "What's the problem?"

The man stubbed his cigarette out, lit another, and recrossed his legs. "The problem is that it's too damned convenient. It's suspicious, especially after your incident in Washington." He pointed with the cigarette. "That reminds me. Bottom left drawer. Something Henry wanted me to get you. A couple things, actually."

Frost bent down and opened the drawer. He smiled. He picked up both objects.

"The knife is just a knife. Nothing special. One piece. Slim. Sturdy. The holster is hand-tooled. Straps are adjustable. Should fit nicely under your suits, built the way you are." Lyle grinned. "Though I don't imagine they're gonna let you carry a pistol in to see Hitler run his mouth."

Frost reached behind his back, under his suit coat, and withdrew the silenced .45 Colt. He removed his jacket and tried the holster on, adjusting the straps here and there. When he had everything fitted and comfortable, he slipped the Colt inside, donned his jacket, and walked to the full-length mirror on the back of the bathroom door.

"See what I mean?" Lyle said. "Can't even see the slightest bulge."

"Not bad," Frost admitted, turning and looking. He walked away from the mirror, back to the dresser, grabbed the small kit with his razor and cream in it. "Are you worried about something specific? With the thing in Washington and the invite coming how it did?"

"That depends." Lyle uncrossed his legs and leaned forward in the chair. "I know you're new at all of this, but did you notice anything during the trip? The same people showing up wherever you were? People being a little too interested in you?"

Frost poked around in his bag, looking for his toothbrush and paste. "Was I being followed, you mean?" Frost thought. "Hard to tell on a train ride that long. You tend to see the same faces every few hours. In the passages and dining car and lounges.”

“True,” Lyle agreed, “but did anyone stare at you? More than would be considered normal?”

Frost shook his head. “I can’t think of anyone behaving that way.”

“And this SS man and his sister?”

“Her name is Ewa,” Frost said, a little testily.

Lyle waved the remark away like a bothersome fly. “Fine. Ewa. Did either Ewa or her brother behave oddly?”

Frost thought back through the trip. The meeting. The dinner. Drinks. Discussion. Could find nothing odd. Except.

“There is a British guy with them. Sir Gerald Thornhill. He seems a bit twitchy, if you know what I mean. Nervous kind of guy. But he didn’t start out that way. At dinner, he was fine to start with. Real calm and cool. But halfway through dinner, he changed.” Frost considered the matter. “Can’t really say why.”

“Anything happen during dinner to cause the change?” Lyle was leaning as far forward as he could without falling off the front of his seat.

“Not that I can think of,” Frost said. “Just your normal discussion between men.”

Lyle nodded, his brow furrowed. He looked down to the spot of floor between his feet.

Frost checked his watch, began emptying his pockets onto the dresser. Wallet. Paper money and loose change. The small scrap of paper he’d gotten from Ewa fell free to the floor, forgotten by Frost for the moment and unseen by either man as it fluttered to rest under the edge of the dresser.

Lyle stood, stubbing his second cigarette out. "I don't much like this, but we do need the invite if you want to meet our man tonight. And since you already secured one…"

"I'm not trying to be reckless here, Lyle," Frost said apologetically. "I'd just prefer to get this done and over with. The longer I'm here, the higher the chance that something else goes wrong. Especially if someone is already on to me."

"You mean the Washington thing? The raid at the Mayflower?"

Frost nodded.

"It's more likely that they were after Greg, Frost. That's what Henry thinks," Lyle said. "He's not exactly unknown."

"That's cryptic."

Lyle shrugged, moved to the door. "Well, like I said. I don't much like using the invite you got, but it's worth a shot." He checked his own watch. "I gotta get moving if I'm gonna leave a flag for our boy."

"A what?"

Lyle stopped, his hand on the doorknob. "A flag. A signal telling our boy that a meet is on. In this case, a chalked mark on a specific lamppost."

"I see."

Lyle opened the door, stopped, turned back. "Make sure you use those wedges Henry gave ya. Rooms here are nice, but the locks are for shit."

Fifteen minutes later, after having walked five blocks north of the hotel and two blocks east, Lyle moved to the edge of the sidewalk, pulled a small piece of chalk from his pocket, and swiped it across the side of a lamppost without breaking stride. He smiled at the execution of the maneuver, thanking God that the drizzle had temporarily subsided while he and Frost had been talking.

———

Forty minutes after Lyle cleared the area, a silver Mercedes rolled slowly toward the lamppost. The man in the back seat, a short balding man with a small, pointed face and thick, circular spectacles, turned his attention outside the vehicle, nonchalantly taking in the people on the street and the scenery in this part of Berlin. He made this trip twice per day. Once in the morning, on the way to the Reich Chancellery, and once each evening, on the way to his home. His eyes tracked along the route, zeroing in on a particular lamppost.

His eyes locked on the target.

The mark was there, just three feet above the base. A single swipe of chalk.

He felt his pulse race. His stomach tightened. Sweat formed in his armpits.

So, the man thought. The meet was on. The Americans had sent someone after all.

11 | Dinner and the Führer

One of the things, Frost thought, that he'd forgotten over the past four years was the simple feeling of pleasure that came with a good, hot shower. There was a relaxation to the practice that left you feeling refreshed and awake, that soothed away the aches and pains that muscles might otherwise retain. His time in the Marines, he reflected as the racing, steamy water raked away the last of the suds and lather, had been almost completely devoid of this luxury. As had his time in the brig.

Frost let the water flow over him for another minute before rotating both handles down and stepping from the shower. He snagged a large, soft towel from a nearby rack, wrapped himself in it, and started the process of shaving, whipping the cream into a foam inside the porcelain cup and then spreading it along and under his jaw with his new horsehair brush. He stopped, wiped steam from the mirror with the side of his hand, and looked at his reflection. He looked at the lather, saw that it did not adequately cover his stubble. Could not think of one good reason to shave it off. Not when he didn't have to.

The hell with it, he told the mirror.

Frost put the razor down, turned on the faucet, and scooped warm water across his face to wash away the shaving cream.

He used a hand towel to dry his face and looked again. He'd never had a beard before. Not in school and certainly not during his time in Shanghai or in the brig. But it was there now. Something like three days' worth of growth covered his jaw, the sides of his face, and his upper lip. He looked…

What?

Older?

No. Something else. Something less refined. Rougher.

Frost finished drying himself, then dressed quickly in the items he'd laid out: a fine black pinstriped suit, white shirt, and black silk tie. He checked the time, looked at himself in the mirror, ran his hands through his hair, and turned his eyes to the .45, the holster, and the pocketknife.

It's just dinner with Ewa, his mind said. Well, dinner and the meeting at the arena. What would you need that for at dinner?

He hefted the .45, felt the weight of it, let his thoughts drift to Ewa. Her eyes. Her smile. Her voice. The nervous laugh that had matched his own for those first few minutes on the train. Her wit. How smoothly she'd trounced him when the discussion had turned to literature.

His feelings for her.

Frost was surprised at the thought. Shocked that he did, in fact, have feelings for her. He knew it. Even Lyle had caught the hint.

She was… What?

Frost didn't know. Couldn't put it into words. But he felt it. In the way his stomach fluttered at the mere thought of her. In remembering how he'd flushed when she'd kissed him goodnight outside her cabin on the train. In the touch of her hands when she'd passed him the note.

Frost dropped the gun on the bed.

The note. He'd not even read it. Had saved it for later. He went to the dresser, to where his clothes from the train were piled. He grabbed them, sorted quickly through them. He found his trousers and dug through the pockets. Nothing.

He stopped, dropped the clothes on the floor, tried to think.

He'd come into the room. He'd turned toward the sitting room. Lyle had been sitting there.

He looked around.

And I emptied my pockets…

Here…

Frost dug through the pile of banknotes and change on the dresser's top. Nothing. No scrap of paper.

He swore to himself and checked his watch again.

He looked around one more time and shook his head, frustrated. If he wanted to be punctual, he needed to get moving.

"Whatever it was," he muttered to the empty room, "she can tell me in half an hour."

Frost walked back to the bed, eyed the weapons again, and decided against them.

What good would they do? he asked himself. They'll get taken away before the speech, and, frankly, if you end up in a situation like that, you're better served to run. Starting a gunfight in the heart of Nazi Germany wasn't something his instructors in the Marines would have called 'an operationally sound idea.' Lamkin, he suspected, would say the same thing, just in a much more colorful way.

———

"What did you tell him, Ewa?"

Ewa cringed. Her brother's voice was hard and even and completely devoid of emotion. It was the voice she hated. The one he'd used to frighten and terrify her for so many years. Her mind drifted back through time, flitting and touching on memories here and there. When he'd been very young and he'd come home with money that wasn't his. And then the watch. And various other intrinsically valuable items. And always with the same scrapes on his knuckles. Then, when he'd been older, there'd been accusations. No consequences. Just the suspicion. The body of a young girl the police had found in the woods near the school. Two other girls, both assaulted. Both raped, but unwilling to point fingers.

And Dieter. Poor Dieter. Their lovable old schnauzer. More silver than black. Ewa remembered what she'd seen. What Fischer had done. What he had been doing when she'd walked into the shed. He'd been thirteen then. Thirteen years old. Covered in blood. Holding a smile and a knife.

"I know about the note, Ewa. I saw you pass it to him," Fischer said. "What was in it? What did it say?"

Ewa raised her head. The face was there, smiling. That thin, knowing smile that he'd always used when he had some sort of advantage to press.

Her face burned, an all-encompassing fire that seemed to originate from everywhere. Blood was running down her face from a gash above one eye. Her lips were both split. A massive bruise was forming on the left side of her face. She could feel it, the hot pressure of fluid and blood building up under the skin. Stretching it. From her eye down to her jawline. The back of her head was sore. She had a wild, pulsing headache that would not subside. That was made worse by the stress. By the yelling.

And by the repeated strikes she kept absorbing.

How many times had he struck her now? Twenty? Thirty?

She swallowed, glared at Elias. Waited to be hit again. Waited for something worse.

She knew where she was. Elias had made no secret of that. She was at Sachsenhausen. At a work camp. At *his* work camp. A place he'd wanted to be assigned. A place where he could beat and whip and torture and kill to his heart's content. A place that was pure, unadulterated evil.

And they would beat her here. They would hit and kick and whip her and, maybe, threaten to gas her here.

Because she hadn't been careful with the note. Because she'd used a note. She swore inwardly, surprising herself. How could she be so stupid? Why hadn't she just told Ridge what she'd learned? Why write it down? Why take that kind of risk?

It didn't matter.

They had her now.

Elias had seen the note. She could try to lie. She'd considered that. Had thought to tell him that the note had been innocuous. Innocent. Just a dinner invitation. A way to contact her in Berlin.

But Elias would not believe something like that.

He'd know if she was lying. He always had in the past. Even when they were little, he'd always known.

And now, because she would not talk, they would beat her.

No. Not her captors. They wouldn't touch her. Would not dare to lay a finger on her. Had not touched her yet.

This, all of this—the eye, the lips, the jaw—was all her brother's doing.

She tried to blink. Tried to speak.

"Why?" Her voice was soft and raspy, and the question was forced out through her clenched teeth.

His hand struck with the speed and vicious accuracy of a pit viper. It bit hard into the swelling on the left side of her face. Her vision exploded with the strike, a million pinpricks of light dancing and jittering before her eyes. Tears were forming and racing freely down her face, and a fresh wave of exquisite pain washed over her, radiating in concentric circles from the point of impact.

"I'm asking the questions here!" Fischer's voice was sharp and hard.

Ewa's breath came in great hitching gasps that set her nerves on edge and sent fresh flares of searing pain rampaging through her skull.

"I'm…" She tried to apologize, but found that the strength to speak was no longer there.

"Now…" Fischer's voice settled slightly, resumed an almost conversational, friendly tone. "What did you tell your American beau?" He pronounced each word of the question clearly and with emphasis, punctuating each one by poking her in the forehead with his index finger.

"Nothing," she gasped, nearly choking on the blood that was streaming from her split lips. "I told him nothing." She tried to spit the blood out, but the effort was frustrated by the searing pain she felt along the side of her face. The blood dribbled out instead, falling onto her chin and dress.

Fischer shifted, scooting his chair to her side. He draped a heavy arm over her shoulders, constricting them with his strength.

She tried to recoil. He squeezed harder.

"Ah, now, my dear Ewa," he chided. "I know you are lying. I have always been able to tell. Even during our childhood. You know this."

She started to protest, but he stopped her, using his free hand to grab her jaw and wrench her face toward his own.

"Don't," he said. "If you try to lie to me, I'll know. And I'll be forced to hurt you again. And you don't want that. Do you?"

She looked at him. He let go of her chin.

"I didn't think so," he said. "Now, I know you told him something. I saw you pass him that note at the hotel. Thornhill saw you pass him that note. That is problematic. For me. For Thornhill. And for the organization we both serve. We need to know what you wrote on that scrap of paper."

Ewa let her head hang low, let the blood dribble and fall. The pain was coursing through her body. With every beat of her heart and every breath. A deep, sharp, thrumming pain. She tried to speak. To say something. Anything.

"What was that, dear sister?"

She tried again. Her voice was barely audible. "Hitler…"

Ewa heard Fischer's chair shift again, saw his feet move into her blurry field of view. She raised her head, looked at him as he squatted in front of her. Saw, through the tears and swelling, a smile on his face that she did not like.

He shook his head slowly. "No, dear sister. Not the Führer, not really. Not even the Nazis. Someone else. Someone bigger. More powerful. Someone next to whom our Führer is but a plaything." He reached out, used his hands to wipe away the tears and grime. Held her jaw in place. "Someone with a vision. And the power to see his vision become reality."

Ewa said nothing. She tried to breathe. Tried to rise above the pain. Tried to think.

"I see you are confused, my dear, sweet Ewa," Fischer said. "What you want to know right now is who is behind this organization. Who runs it? What is it called?" He smiled at her again. "That, I am afraid, is something I cannot tell you. It is immaterial to our present conversation. What is important, what I really need to know, is what you told your darling Captain Frost. Can you tell me that? What did you tell your little American spy?"

Ewa did not try to speak. She sat there, her jaw clutched in Elias's hand, and tried to ignore the pain. Tried to stop the tears.

Fischer clicked his tongue. "I thought so. It's unfortunate that you are so unwilling to help me. I believe that I will just have to ask him myself."

He released his hold on her face and she saw his blurred form turn and move away. She saw him grow small and dark in the shadows at the edge of her consciousness. She heard him speaking, though she could not make out his words. He appeared to turn toward her. Appeared to nod.

A flash of excruciating pain erupted from a point on the back of her skull. Her vision, what was left of it, went white. Then orange. Then black.

———

The man from Paris picked up his target as he left the hotel, following on foot and keeping well back as the American made several turns. He kept his hands in his pockets, one of them fingering the small .25 Walther he prayed he would not need. He kept his collar turned up against the gray drizzle that was just tapering off again. The hat on his head—a flat cap of thick wool—was pulled low across his brow, hiding most of his face.

The target was moving quickly, dodging other pedestrians here and whipping around corners there. Not a surveillance detection run, the man from Paris thought. Just a man in a hurry. Confident and comfortable in his surroundings. And likely trying to stay as dry as was possible during the short journey.

The target paused, looked left and right, crossed the moderately busy street in front of him, and ducked into an alley. The man from Paris did the same, without hurrying or rushing. Losing sight of the target wasn't something to get excited about. Not right now. Not for this part of the job. He did, after all, know exactly where the target was heading.

—

Horcher was as elegant a restaurant as Frost had ever set foot in. The floor was dotted with small, intimate tables, each of which was covered with a fine linen tablecloth, gold-trimmed china, tall crystal wine glasses, and a small bowl of impossibly red roses. The walls, difficult to see in the low, secretive lighting, were a burnt orange color, offset by intricate walnut-colored trim, tall olive draperies, and twenty sets of French double doors leading to a small atrium. The food, what he'd seen as he waited, was nothing short of spectacular. The main course this evening appeared to be a row of succulent lamb chops, asparagus spears, and mashed potatoes covered in some sort of reduction that Frost couldn't even begin to describe.

He tugged at his sleeve and exposed the face of his watch. Quarter past six o'clock, it read. Ewa was late. Frost put the sleeve back into place, lifted the small cup of black coffee the waiter had brought eight minutes earlier, and surveyed the room as he sipped.

The restaurant was full of sounds, the way most places like it seemed to be. There was the usual collection of voices that filled the room. Various conversations. Some loud and boisterous. Some subdued and private. There was the tinkling noise that always seemed to come with dining out. Cubed ice against crystal glass. Knives and forks against bone china.

There was also a string quartet, off in the far corner of the room. A cello. A bass. Two violins. They were not yet playing, but simply tuning and adjusting their instruments, delicately twisting pegs, rosining bows, checking the angles of chin rests and endpin holders.

It was, Frost thought, so oddly normal. Here he was, recently booted out of the United States Marine Corps, sitting in one of Berlin's most popular restaurants, surrounded by a large contingent of men in uniform who would, if the newspapers had it right, soon be at war. And yet, there was no sign of that here. It was simply dinnertime in one of the world's largest cities.

So very odd, he thought again. He tried to dismiss the feeling as he sat and sipped at his coffee. He resisted the urge to check his watch again and kept looking toward the front doors, waiting for Ewa.

A familiar face wearing a familiar uniform appeared there, spoke to the maître d', and began weaving his way through the restaurant.

Frost stood, stuck a hand out. "Guten Abend, Herr Fischer."

Fischer took the hand, shook it warmly. "Ewa told me you would be here," he said.

Frost offered Fischer a seat. Fischer declined. "Bad news, I'm afraid. My sister sent me to tell you that she is not feeling well. A bit under the weather, as you would say. Something she picked up on the train, no doubt. Hit her quite hard."

Frost felt his heart race, but could not exactly say why. Concern, he supposed. "I'm sorry to hear that. Will she be okay? Is there anything I can do?"

Fischer waved a hand dismissively. "It is nothing serious. A head cold of some sort. It will pass, and she is being looked after by very capable people. She asked me to come here to let you know. I daresay she did not want you worrying."

"I appreciate that. I do hope she feels better soon."

"I am sure she will," Fischer said. "Now, as for you, I have something for you. Something you might enjoy. A little surprise for a new friend." He glanced down at his own watch. "It is a little early, but…"

"But what?"

"Well, since dinner has been ruined for you, I wonder if you might wish to accompany me to the arena?" Fischer looked nervous. "You see, I have some friends I would like you to meet before the Führer's speech tonight. Friends and benefactors. Individuals who are very high up in the Nazi party. People to whom I owe a great deal." Fischer began listing names.

Frost recognized some of the names. Some were completely foreign to him. But the fourth name…

He'd heard it only once before. From Henry Jackson. The man Henry had sent him here for. The man code-named "Locksmith".

Frost's mind raced. Thought about a possible rendezvous with Locksmith that very evening. Arranged by the man in front of him. It was supposed to appear random, he told himself. That had been Henry's intent. And Lyle's. A step up beside the right person. The correct, seemingly innocent phrases spoken back and forth in the proper sequence. And then a short walk elsewhere for a more substantial conversation and, hopefully, the passing of a file. Technical research from Uranverein.

But if you're introduced to the man? If Fischer walks you right to him and you shake his hand? Can you work the proper phrases into that kind of conversation?

Yes.

I could be done with this job tonight, Frost told himself. Could be in possession of the dossier in a few minutes.

What then? Just jump on the next train out of Berlin? Back to Paris?

And what about Ewa?

Damnit, Frost. Focus on the job. Forget the girl.

But he couldn't.

Frost blinked, saw that Fischer was peering at him, waiting for an answer. He smiled, clicked his heels together in the way he'd seen Fischer do it, and offered a short bow. "Herr Fischer, I'd be honored."

"Very good." Fischer grinned. He dug into a pocket, dropped cash on the table over Frost's protestations, and turned to the door. "Please, follow me."

12 | Red Carpet

The drive from Horcher to the arena took the better part of twenty minutes by Frost's watch. He sat in the backseat of a car with Fischer, while the driver, a short man in a dark suit and a flat, woolen cap, navigated the streets of Berlin. Frost found himself staring out the window, trying to take in as much as possible. They passed a dizzying array of buildings and landmarks and memorials. Some Frost recognized. From pictures in the papers. Stories he'd read. Politics. Government. And the 1936 Olympiad. Most places he did not recognize. And everything, every office and storefront, seemed to be hung with long, red banners and a black swastika enclosed in a pristine white disc.

"The Führer says that flag is a symbol of our struggle," Fischer offered. "A rise from the past. From our humiliation in the wake of the Great War to our new place in the world. Victory of our social ideas."

Frost turned. "You buy that?"

Fischer shrugged. "Why not?" he said, his voice distant. "It's as good as any explanation can be." He looked at Frost. "It is odd, don't you think? That the men who create such banners always have such lofty ideas about them. Such elaborate explanations." He turned back to the window and gestured with his chin, a short jerk toward the outside. "In the end, it's just fabric. Just fabric arranged in a certain way. Look at your own flag. Stars and stripes. A star for every state. Stripes of different colors, each with some meaning that doesn't translate well when you are the man down in the trenches."

Frost returned his gaze to the scenery flashing by. "Well put."

"It's all nonsense, really, Herr Frost. You know it and so do I. Men do not fight for a flag or a banner. They do not even fight because they are told to do so. That is only why they go to where the fighting is, or will be. Why they travel there. Because of the orders. But the actual fighting. The taking of another's life and the sacrificing of one's own? No, that fighting is done for much simpler reasons. For their brothers. For the man next to them. And, for some of the more enlightened among us, for ideas."

"Is that why you wear the uniform?" Frost asked, watching out the window as a monument to something drifted past.

"If I have my history correct," Fischer said, "we were both raised in depressions. Parents out of work. Economies in ruin. Lines for food. I've seen these things. I've stood in the lines. I know what it is to be poor. Not just penniless. But possession-less. To have nothing but a pile of rubble and a few scraps of moldy bread. You too, yes?"

Frost nodded, recalled the farm. The barren fields where his father had once grown various crops. The empty barn where the tractors and horses had once been stowed.

"That's why I wear the uniform, Herr Frost," Fischer said. "So that I never have to experience that again."

"It's hard to believe there was a war here twenty years ago," Frost offered. "It's impressive how far you've come."

The city was strikingly beautiful, he thought. Even with the banners hanging from every surface. It reminded him of the time his mother had taken the family to Indianapolis so that he and Randolph could see the Fourth of July fireworks. The American flag had been everywhere then. Hanging from buildings. Protruding from porches. Red, white, and blue bunting slung along every fence and façade.

"Looks like the Fourth back home."

"The Fourth?" Fischer asked. "Ah, yes. Your Independence Day." He paused. "If I remember correctly, some of my countrymen fought in that war."

"True," Frost said, "but for the other side."

"Pardon?"

"The British hired German mercenaries to fight for them back then. We got help from the French. Your predecessors were on the wrong side then." Frost followed the comment with a roguish grin and a chuckle.

Fischer answered it in kind. "Kind of hard to know things like that ahead of time. What is it you Americans say? Hindsight is perfect?"

"Hindsight is twenty-twenty," Frost corrected. "Close enough."

"Such a nice turn of phrase," Fischer said. "I think I'll keep that one handy. Ah. We are here."

The car rolled to a stop at the curb and the driver leapt out, rounded the front of the car, and opened the door for Fischer and Frost to exit. Fischer stepped out of the car first. Frost followed.

The scene at the arena was pure madness, like nothing he'd ever seen. The same Nazi banners he'd seen throughout the drive graced a stone façade that rose more than one hundred feet in the air. Floodlights were positioned at the base of each banner, projecting massive columns of brilliant light into a sky that was finally clearing of rain and drizzle. The crowd was immense, loud and surging. A human wave encroached on the scene, parted down the middle by a single, five-foot-wide roll of red carpet. In the screaming crowd—many of whom wore uniforms of some sort—Frost saw that nearly every person clutched a small replica of the Nazi flag. They were waving the flags madly and the effect was impressive. A huge, undulating wave that rolled toward Frost before crashing back on itself. Somewhere, hidden, a band was playing an upbeat march that Frost did not recognize, the brassy notes clear and drifting through the cool evening air.

"It's like Indy," Frost muttered.

"What's that?" Fischer was at his shoulder, smiling and waving at the crowd.

Frost turned, nearly had to yell to be heard. "Like Indy. A big motorcar race we have every year in Indianapolis. Five hundred miles, with two hundred thousand fans screaming and waving their hats and all." Frost stopped to take a breath. "It's the only time I've ever seen anything like this."

Fischer took Frost by the elbow and ushered him onto the edge of the red carpet. "Trust me, Herr Frost. You've never seen anything like this."

Frost froze in place when he realized what Fischer intended. He was going right up through the middle of the crowd. Along the same red carpet that Hitler might—would, he thought—

walk down later. Right through the loudest and most ardent portion of the screaming masses.

Fischer leaned in, a huge grin splitting his face. "I hope you don't mind, but I took certain liberties in planning this."

Frost stared at Fischer. He worked hard to remain steady, had to think to prevent his knees from shaking.

"As I said, I have some people you must meet. And they wish to meet you."

"Why?"

A gallant shrug. "We get common folk emigrating here all the time. Menial laborers. Cleaners. People who can do little more than operate a shovel or lift a rifle. But engineers? No. Scientists? Not unless they are originally from the Fatherland. You are something of a curiosity. And, on that note, plus the fact that my sister seems to think quite highly of you, I put in a few good words on your behalf. As I said before, we must find something useful for you to do. Something commensurate with your skills and talents." Fischer's grin changed to something else. Something decidedly different. He leaned closer, almost conspiratorially close. "I even got you a private meeting with the Führer himself."

Jesus Christ, Frost thought. He's going to take me in front of Hitler? He wouldn't joke about something like that, would he?

Fischer tugged at Frost's sleeve, and Frost began walking a few steps behind him up the carpet toward the main entrance. He forced a smile onto his face and hoped it hid the panic he felt. He waved. Occasionally, he stopped to shake someone's offered hand. He looked ahead, to where Fischer was doing the same.

Holy hell, Frost thought. How did I get myself into this?

Relax. It'll be over soon. Just follow the man in there. Meet Hitler. More importantly, meet Locksmith. Exchange the code phrases about the weather and holidays in Italy, collect whatever information he has, and get the hell out of Germany.

And what about Ewa?

Stop thinking about Ewa. She's not the job. And you've known her for, what? Less than two days? It's not like you're in love with her.

Frost felt his heart lurch.

Are you?

He felt his breath catch in his throat.

Jesus, Ridge. Really? Just like that? Some girl smooches you once, on the cheek, and you're ready to propose marriage? What the hell is wrong with you?

He kept moving toward the entrance, wishing Ewa was on the carpet with him. Feeling that she belonged there. Needed to be there.

Stop thinking crazy shit, Frost.

But it's not crazy, he told himself. Yes, he'd known her for two days. But…damn. He wanted her here, on the carpet. Close. Holding his hand.

Did Germans do that in public?

Would you even care?

Frost's feet began moving faster, more comfortably, eating up the remainder of the red carpet between where he was and where he was heading. He wondered how Ewa was feeling, hoped that she wouldn't be sick for very long. He wanted to see her again. Needed to. And soon.

And what happens then? What happens if you get what you need tonight? What happens when the job—he couldn't bring himself to call it a mission—is over and you need to get the hell out of Germany? Are you planning to take her with you? Just going to waltz in like Fred Astaire and sweep her off her feet and back to America?

Would she even go?

Frost met Fischer at the top of the arena's wide, fan-shaped stairs. Fischer clapped Frost on the shoulder and conducted him through the doors.

Frost swallowed, or tried to. He realized his mouth was dry. His nerves were slightly frazzled by the gauntlet he'd just walked and the thoughts rampaging through his head. He followed Fischer around a corner, away from the foyer, trying to sort through the avalanche of feelings crashing down on him.

She thinks you've come here to stay, his mind told him.

Why do you care? She's just a girl. Just one girl. There are thousands like her back home. Maybe more.

He followed Fischer down a wide passage, barely noticing the elaborate decorations. All but ignoring the ornate vases and tables and draperies and paintings.

But she's not like other girls. You won't find anyone like her back home.

Damnit, he swore at himself. Get a grip, Ridge.

Job first.

Girl second.

Fischer swept around another corner, pushed his way through a side door flanked by troopers in the slim black uniform of the SS. When the soldiers moved to bar Frost's passage, Fischer issued a curt order and continued walking.

"He is with me."

The soldiers stood aside and Frost entered the new hallway, noting the stark contrast between this hall and the one he'd just passed through. There were no banners here. No lights or flowers or paintings or mirrors. Just harsh overhead lighting, concrete floors and walls, and an array of pipes and valves of varying sizes lining the left-hand wall.

A maintenance hall.

"Hurry, Herr Frost," Fischer said. "They are waiting."

Frost caught up, saw that his host appeared to be heading to a door at the far end of the hall.

"You didn't need to do this," Frost said. "I'll be content to keep my head down and do my work."

Fischer stopped in front of the door. Nodded at one of the guards. "Nonsense. We can't have you digging ditches, can we? How would we look if we wasted your talents making you do something that any idiot can do?"

The guards moved away from the door when Fischer reached for the handle, their heels clicking on the rough concrete and the sound echoing down the length of the hall.

Frost tensed at the noise, became aware that he could no longer hear the crowds or the band. All that was left was the nearly unbroken silence in the hall.

The door clicked under Fischer's hand. It moved inward. Fischer stood to one side, waving Frost into the room beyond. "Guests first, Herr Frost."

Frost stepped to the door, felt his blood run cold. The fine hairs on the back of his neck stood on end. He felt his skin tighten there. Felt his jaw clench. Felt a single bead of ice-cold sweat form and trickle down his temple. He looked at

Fischer, examined the face, saw none of the warmth there he had become used to. Saw, instead… What?

Something is wrong, his mind screamed. Something is very badly wrong.

But what?

Frost placed his hand on the door, pushed. The door swung away, giving him access to a room that was completely dark. Frost's hand reached automatically for the light switch that had to be on the wall beside the door. His fingers found it, pressed the top button. A single, bare bulb flooded the room with white, incandescent light. Frost's eyes narrowed at the insult. His hand came up to block the searing brightness as he blinked away the tears that had formed involuntarily. A picture began to materialize in front of him. A man. Seated in a chair.

Shirtless.

And bloody.

With his head hanging low, his chin resting on his own bare chest. Frost eyed the man, saw the strips of flesh hanging loose. Saw the puddle of blood collecting at the base of the chair. Saw the splattering further away.

The smell hit him full in the face, assaulted his nasal passages. A smell he knew well. Urine. Feces. And the rotten, burnt odor of seared flesh.

Dear God. What in the hell…

Before Frost could say anything, Fischer moved past him, hurried to the man in the chair, knelt in front of him. Slapped him playfully in the face.

"Wake up, my friend," he chided. "Wake up. Someone is here to see you."

The man in the chair did not wake. He did groan, a long, grating, piteous sound that set Frost's nerves on edge.

Frost felt glued to the concrete floor. His mind was screaming at him. Telling him to run. To bowl over the guards and race off down the hall. To charge into the crowds. To leave. To go somewhere else. Anywhere else.

"Ah." Fischer stood and moved to the man's side. "I feared as much. My friend here is quite unconscious, as you can see. We have been trying to get him to talk for some time." Fischer shrugged, looked at Frost. "Won't even tell us who he really is or who he is working for."

Frost swallowed hard. "That's unfortunate." He looked around. "Listen, Elias, maybe we should—"

"In due time, Herr Frost. In due time." Fischer reached down and grabbed the man by the hair. He yanked backward, lifting the face into the light.

Frost gasped. The nose had been shattered. One eye was swollen shut. Blood from a series of cuts and abrasions was pouring down the face.

But the face was recognizable. Frost knew it, even though he'd never been this close to the man. He remembered it from the file Henry Jackson had forced him to memorize.

"I think," Fischer said, "that you might know this man."

Frost tried to ignore the face. He tried to keep his own impassive.

Fischer let the head drop. Blood and sweat dribbled down from the various wounds. Strings of saliva trailed from his mouth, stretching, sagging. Falling onto the man's bare chest and soiled trousers. Fischer shook his head. He collected a rag from a table nearby and used it to wipe his hands clean.

When he was finished, he tossed the rag onto the man's lap and leveled his gaze at Frost.

"I believe, Herr Frost," Fischer said, "that you know this man simply as Locksmith."

Frost lunged backward, his mind racing, panicked. He started trying to calculate. To remember. How far to the foyer? How far to the hotel? How many guards had he seen?

He couldn't remember. He cursed himself.
He'd not been paying attention. His mind had been elsewhere. On the sights. On the sounds.
On Ewa.
How stupid.

He started to turn, made it only one-quarter of the way around before two sets of large, strong hands grabbed him from behind. One set held him up and in place, his feet barely touching the floor. The other set worked quickly to lock his hands down and behind him. Frost struggled, tried to gain purchase with his feet. Against the nearest wall. Against the thighs of the men behind him. But nothing worked. The more he struggled the tighter they held him. He felt the cold of the steel lock around one wrist, then the other.

"Right now, you are wondering how I knew." Fischer smiled thinly, his voice even and cruel and smug. "The answer is that I didn't. Not completely. Not until I saw my darling sister pass you that note outside your hotel." He paused, leering. "I asked her about it several times, but she would not answer. She forced us to do terrible things to her. Things I would not wish on another human being."

Frost flushed with anger, lunged against his restraints, was slammed to the ground and pinned there with one knee at the base of his skull and one astride his hips.

"You son of a bitch!" Frost growled, his face pressed into the hard concrete.

"Now, now, Herr Frost. Such vulgarity. And I thought you a gentleman. I do hope that you remember your manners in front of dear Ewa. It would be a shame for her to find out who, and what, you really are." He paused and chuckled. "Oh, that's right. I've already told her. Already let her know that her precious Ridge is a filthy American spy."

The guards stepped off of him and began to lift him by his handcuffs. Frost gritted his teeth against the pain in his shoulders. "Where is she? What have you—"

Fischer moved swiftly, slamming his knee into the side of Frost's head. A flash of yellow light exploded in Frost's consciousness and he sagged against the men holding him.

"Not now, Herr Frost," Fischer said. "You will see her again quite soon. As a matter of fact, she is waiting for you just a few kilometers from here. But first…"

Frost opened his mouth to curse again. Tried to twist his body against the grips of the men holding him partially upright. A searing pain blasted through his skull. Waves of pain shot through every part of his being as his vision went white and then black.

13 | Extraction

The voice in Frost's head seemed to come from a great distance, and the words penetrated his consciousness slowly. Out of order. All drawn and distorted and wrong.

"Ridge, can you hear me?"

Frost tried to open his eyes, but they would not move. They were heavy and slothful and refused to acknowledge any form of subservience to his central nervous system.

"Ridge…"

The voice was there again. Hovering. Pleading. Lurking off in the dark recesses of his mind, beneath the fog and the waves of pain that seemed to course from a point at the rear of his skull.

My head, he thought. I hit it.

No. Not right. I got hit. Something struck me. From behind.

Frost tried to focus on the pain, to isolate it, but the effort proved beyond him. The waves were spreading and flowing. Moving beyond his skull. To his shoulders and back and down the length of both arms.

The voice drifted in again, loomed there in the forefront of his thoughts. But he could not latch onto it. Could not hold it steady. Each time he got close, it would waft away.

Like smoke, he thought. Or wisps of steam.

Frost tried to calm his body, to steady his thoughts. He took a deep breath in and exhaled slowly.

The click disturbed him. Something in his brain announced that it was the sound of a door lock being undone. A creaking followed, and his mind decided that it was the sound of poorly maintained hinges. The steps came next. The precise and measured tread of boots on concrete. Something he remembered from his own past.

"Elias…" the voice said. "Why?"

A sharp slapping noise followed, accompanied by a short, nearly inaudible gasp.

Ewa, Frost thought. The voice was Ewa's. But wrong somehow. Muffled. Altered. As if she was speaking through a mouthful of cotton.

But why?

Frost tried to force his eyelids to open and failed. He pushed at the corners of his mind, tried to force it to take in details. Tried to examine his body from the inside out.

His head ached, a deep, dull pounding that occasionally broke out into stabbing pains. A soreness existed, starting at a spot behind and below his right ear. His shoulders burned, the muscles there aflame and…

Bent?

Yes.

His arms were wrenched back against the joints and tied down. Over something stiff. The back of his chair? Yes. He concentrated on the feelings, tried to move his arms and felt the harsh bite of something firmly encircling each wrist. He pulled gingerly, felt the biting grow sharper and knew that his wrists were bound, separately, so that he could not use one hand to free the other. They had been fastened to the slats at the back of his chair with thin bands of wire.

Frost fought the urge to panic. Somewhere to his left he could hear a faint sobbing.

Ewa!

Not now, he told himself. Not now. Keep searching.

He returned to his survey, tried to move his legs and found them immobile. He felt the same sharp bite at the top of each thigh and at the thin, bony part of each ankle.

Frost tried to open his eyes again and partially succeeded. He felt the crust of sleep break away from one eye and tried to blink it clear.

"Ah, very good. We are awake."

A scraping noise that Frost identified as a chair being dragged across the floor cut through the thick fog in his mind. Boots appeared, blurry, in his field of view. A hand grabbed Frost's jaw and lifted it.

"No. No. No. That won't do at all. How many times have I told them? My prisoners must be able to see." The hand on Frost's jaw gripped tighter and his limited vision was soon obscured by a fuzzy, crimson blob.

The rag was rough and the hand that rubbed it across Frost's eyes was rougher still, but when it was removed, Frost could see.

"Elias," he muttered.

"Guten Morgen, Herr Frost." Fischer was seated in a chair facing him, smiling at him, his eyes peering into Frost's own. "You'll have a concussion, I'm afraid. Headaches and maybe some nausea for the time being, but no permanent damage."

He shrugged. "At least, that is what the doctors say. What the hell would I know?" He slapped Frost's bound thigh and a short bark of pain shot up Frost's leg. "Oh. I'm so sorry. Did that hurt?"

Frost bit off his reply. Said nothing.

"You know, I was just telling our dear Ewa over there how lucky you were to have just a concussion. It could have been much worse. You could have run, for example. You could have run, and my guards would have been forced to shoot you. And where would that leave us?"

Again, Frost did not respond. He just glared at Fischer.

"I'll tell you. Nowhere. It would have left us nowhere. I would just have a dead spy on my hands. And dead men are such bores. You cannot talk to them. You cannot hurt them. You cannot find out what they know or what they were doing."

Frost tried to turn his head to look to his left, to where Ewa was supposed to be, to where the sobs were coming from.

"I wouldn't do that," Fischer advised. "You have some very serious swelling along your neck. Right about here."

Fischer leaned forward and grabbed Frost in a collar tie, squeezing the back of his neck and sending a lightning bolt of pain through his muscles and brain.

Frost bit off the scream, clenched his jaw against the pain.

Fischer leered at him, squeezed harder. Frost trembled beneath the effort, but did not utter so much as a single grunt.

Fischer released his grasp. He eyed Frost for several seconds. Then, he laughed and shook his finger at Frost.

"They were right about you," he said. "I didn't believe them, but they were right about you. Don't expect him to break easily. That's what they told me. American Marines don't break easily. They don't feel pain. Not the way normal human beings do. They don't react the same way."

Frost stared back at Fischer. Sweat started to form on his face and back. He felt himself breathing hard.

Fischer stood, waved a hand in the air as though dismissing the advice of his colleagues. He walked to a small, stainless-steel table and began rooting through items laid out on top of it. "It's nonsense, though. The idea that you do not feel pain. That you are, ah, unbreakable. Everyone feels pain. Everyone. It is a simple matter of finding the proper vector." He paused, turned back to Frost. "That is the proper term, yes? Vector. Direction and magnitude, yes?"

He went back to sorting through the objects on the table. Frost heard the distinctive sound of metal scraping against metal.

"You see, Herr Frost, I think that I could poke and prod you all day long and that you would not say a single word to me. I even believe that I could skin you, the way I skinned Herr Locksmith, and you might not even grace me with a single scream. And why?" He turned from the table, holding a large scalpel in his hands. "Simple. Because while the magnitude may be correct, the direction is not. And breaking someone is all about magnitude and direction. Just like in engineering, yes?"

Frost said nothing. His eyes tracked the end of the scalpel.

"In your case, the direction is, ah, shall we say…elsewhere. I simply need to apply the proper magnitude to someone else. To someone you care for. Ewa, for example."

Fischer moved to his right, to Frost's left, to where the sobbing had just ceased. He chuckled. "Now, I daresay, were I to elicit a scream from darling Ewa here, you would answer my questions. Wouldn't you?"

Frost forced his head to turn against the swelling pain, choked down the grunt that tried to escape his lips. He saw Ewa, tied to a chair maybe ten feet away. Saw her face. The sweat. The tears. The blood. The terror. Frost strained against the wires holding him in place, felt the slicing, fiery pain as the thin cabling chewed into his wrists and ankles. Watched helplessly as Fischer moved nearer to Ewa. Saw him grasp a handful of her hair and yank Ewa's head back and to the side.

Ewa screamed as the scalpel bit into her swollen cheek. Frost watched as Fischer drew the scalpel down along her cheekbone to a point just above her jawline. Blood poured freely from the wound. Fischer turned to Frost and grinned lecherously.

"Ah, yes," he said. "I knew that would get a reaction out of you." He released his grasp on Ewa's hair, letting her head fall. He walked to Frost, stopped in front of him, sat down again in his chair. He leaned forward, close enough to tap the scalpel on Frost's knee to pull his attention away from Ewa. "Now, this is how we will proceed. I will tell you what I know. I will tell you what I suspect. I will ask you questions. If you lie to me, or if I believe that you are trying to mislead me, well…" He shrugged and looked over at his bleeding, crying sister.

"You're an asshole."

"I've been called worse." Fischer laughed, then abruptly became serious. "Who sent you?"

Frost said nothing. His mind was busy. He tried to gauge and weigh his options. What might this lunatic already know? What might Locksmith have told him? Was there someone else who had talked?

The last thought caught Frost off guard. Of course someone had talked. Of course there had been a leak. They'd been on to him in Washington, hadn't they?

So where was the leak? *Who* was the leak?

Did it matter right now?

"Shall I cut her again?" Fischer was staring at him, one eyebrow cocked up. He let his face relax and sighed. "Oh, that's right. I did promise to tell you what I know and suspect, didn't I?"

Fischer stood, returned the scalpel to the table, wiped his hands clean, and came back to his chair with a thin file in his hands. He flipped it open and smiled at Frost. "You are Everett Frost, known by your friends as either Ridge or just Frost. You are from a small town in Indiana…" His voice trailed off as he flipped through several pages. "Ah. Yes. Garrett, Indiana. You have a father, Dorsey, deceased. A mother, Bernice, also deceased. And a brother, Randolph. Again, deceased. Randolph, if my information is correct, followed you into the United States Marine Corps and was killed in action in 1937 when your own commander, a Brigadier General Albert Whitehead, opened fire on a bridge you and your team were crossing in Shanghai, China."

At the mention of Randolph, Frost strained again at his bindings, felt the wires cut into his flesh, felt the trickle of warm blood.

"Fuck you," he growled.

Fischer was watching him with something akin to clinical disinterest. As if he could care less how much Frost struggled or what vulgarities flew from his lips.

And why should he care? He has everything he needs. Information and a way to pry more from you. And you, you dumbass leatherneck, walked right into all of this. Just as naïve as can be. A babe in the woods.

Goddamnit.

"Anyway," Fischer flipped some pages in the file, "you spent some time in the brig in Pearl Harbor after a physical altercation with this General Whitehead. You were very recently released from your imprisonment and discharged from the Marine Corps at the behest of a group calling themselves the Federal Trade Committee." Fischer closed the file and set it on the floor next to him. "But this group, this Federal Trade Committee, does not really exist. Not for anything to do with trade. According to my source," he offered a thin, proud smile, "this group, called Unit Twelve, exists for the sole purpose of conducting intelligence operations in, shall we say, denied territory. You were, if my sources are to be believed, their first major operation. A single asset sent deep into the heart of Nazi Germany to pull out information relating to our atomic weapons research."

Fischer stood, began pacing. "And that is where I am confused. What would a simple Marine know about atomic weapons? Why send you?"

Frost thought about staying silent, but chose not to. "Because I was available. That's all."

Fischer hustled back to his chair. Sat down. "I would love to believe that. In other circumstances, I almost could believe that. If, say, you were sent here to steal Panzer blueprints or something similar, I could almost believe that this Unit Twelve would send the first warm body they could recruit. But atomic weapons information?" Fischer shook his head. "No, Herr Frost. That cannot be true. There must be another reason they sent you."

Frost gritted his teeth against the pains wracking his body. To his left he could hear Ewa whimpering.

"Are you going to tell me, or shall I hurt her again?"

"You didn't ask me a question."

"Why send you?"

Frost shifted as best he could. "You said it yourself. I'm just a warm body."

Fischer shook his head, stood, headed for the table. "I don't think so, Herr Frost. I think you just lied to me. I let one slide, but…" He picked up the scalpel, looked at it, and moved toward Ewa. She tried to scream when he grabbed her face. Tried to move it away from his grasp.

"Tell me, Herr Frost. Tell me or I slice her open again." Fischer pointed the scalpel at Ewa, let it hover over her wounded cheek. Touched it to the open gash.

She shrieked.

"Stop!" Frost yelled. "Jesus Christ, stop."

Fischer turned. "Yes?"

"Physics," Frost said. "I studied physics in college."

Fischer turned away from Ewa and moved closer to Frost, eyeing him warily. He looked confused. His face was contorted into a mask of disbelief. Then, it cleared.

"Gott im Himmel," he said. "You are quite serious."

"It was only because I studied physics."

"Because you might understand? Not because you are working on the same type of weapons?" Fischer seemed shocked.

Frost looked at him curiously, careful to hide what he was thinking, what he'd been told about Szilard and Einstein. "What?"

"You have nothing to do with Einstein or Szilard? Have no knowledge of this letter they have sent to Roosevelt?"

"I don't know who Szilard is," Frost snapped. "And I don't know shit about any letter."

Fischer went to the table, put the scalpel down, and began pacing back and forth behind the array of instruments. He started muttering to himself.

"Was ist, wenn er die Wahrheit sagt? Was ist, wenn Thornhill recht hat?"

Frost caught part of the question, translated it quickly. *What if I'm telling the truth? Was Thornhill right?* "Thornhill? What the hell does Thornhill have to do with this?"

Fischer ignored Frost's question and kept pacing, faster now, almost panicked. Kept muttering. "Das ist nicht möglich."

"What?" Frost yelled. "What's not possible?"

Fischer froze in place, turned to Frost. His eyes were wide. There was something there Frost hadn't seen before. There was…

Fear.

Whatever conclusion he'd just come to terrified him.

Oh, shit.

Fischer moved closer to the table, steadied himself. Frost saw him swallow. Saw perspiration forming on his temples. Saw him step away from the table. He moved around it, his right hand lowering to his side and unclipping the top of the black leather holster there. He drew the weapon, a Luger, and stopped four paces from Frost, just behind the chair. He pointed the barrel straight at Frost's head and Frost had to stop himself flinching.

"Where did you first meet Thornhill?" Fischer's voice shook. Whether it was with fury or terror, Frost did not know and did not much care.

"On the train," Frost said. "With you."

"Liar!" Fischer screamed. He inched forward, his boots scraping along the floor. He jabbed the gun at Frost. "When did you first meet him? Was it Shanghai?"

"What the hell are you talking about?" Frost barked.

Fischer's voice was shaking now. The gun in his hand trembled. "Did you talk to Thornhill in Shanghai?"

"I don't understand…"

The gun went off, the explosion of the shot deafening in the small room. Ewa screamed. Frost felt the pressure wave as the bullet passed by his right ear.

"Answer my question!" Fischer yelled. "Answer me or the next bullet goes right into her brain."

"No. I never met Thornhill before," Frost said. "I never met him. Never talked to him. Never even laid eyes on—"

"Liar!" Fischer squeezed off another round.

It exploded in a spray of sparks between Frost's feet.

"You know about Thornhill and you know about VEIL. You know about Resh. Was it Resh who sent you? Was it?" Fischer was still yelling.

Frost was doing everything possible to keep his wits about him. His mind leapt around at the speed of light, trying to track in on whatever the hell had gone wrong in the last sixty seconds.

Fischer knew about Unit 12. There's a leak, but that's irrelevant right now. He asked about atomic weapons. Seemed to believe you about having no knowledge of an American project. Then he snapped. He snapped and started asking questions about Thornhill. Seems to think you know about some society. Seems to think you know the man. That you met in Shanghai. And someone named Resh? But…

Frost's mind flashed backward through time. Saw the assault on the warehouse. Saw the bodies of the principal objectives. Heard Randolph's voice.

"Christ, sir. This fella here is white."

Saw the man's face. Younger then. Fewer worry lines. Compared it to Thornhill. Recalled the way Brit had flinched on the train when Shanghai and the 4th Marines had been mentioned.

Holy shit.

"Who the hell is Thornhill? Who's Resh? What's VEIL?" Frost asked.

Fischer shook his head. A thin, terrified smile worked its way across his face. He turned, pointed the gun at Ewa.

Frost lurched forward against his restraints. "No!"

14 | Unbound

The explosion threw Frost backward. He slammed into the room's rear wall, bounced off it, and crashed to the floor on his back. Pieces of the door's heavy hinges and locking mechanism bounced and skittered around him. He could hear nothing except the pounding in his skull and a high-pitched whine in his ears. He could see nothing but the imprint the flash had made on each of his retinas. His whole body ached. The wires at his wrists and ankles bit hard into his flesh. The room spun. Frost shook his head, trying to clear it, felt the pain in his neck flare up again. He welcomed it. It helped to center his thoughts.

He blinked his eyes, tried to clear them, to peer through the smoke and haze. The ringing in his ears subsided slightly. His eyes watered. The lights in the room were out. A few small fires burned, offering brief flickers of light. Parts of the door, he thought. Bits of paper. The dossier.

Frost heard groans in the dark. One close by that was somehow feminine and another, further away, past his feet, that wasn't.

He started to turn his neck again, trying to locate Ewa. She had to be here somewhere. Had to be the nearer voice.

Frost stopped turning his neck when the figures appeared in the doorway. Four of them, he thought. Four men entering the room silently, like malevolent ghosts. One turning right. One left. And one in the middle. The fourth simply turned and crouched just inside the space where the door had been.

"Two minutes," a muffled voice said. In English.

The man in the middle of the room nodded, appeared to turn his head from side to side. "Search the bodies. The American and the girl go with us."

"And the Nazi?"

There was a short silence. "Kill him. He is useless to us now."

The men began moving around, backlit by the small fires. Frost became aware that they were carrying short rifles or submachine guns, but couldn't make out the type.

He coughed and gagged. "Over here."

One of the shadowy figures moved closer. Knelt over him. Leaned close. He was wearing a mask, Frost saw. A knit cap that covered everything but the eyes and mouth.

"I have the American."

"The girl, too," added a second voice. "Need a second to patch her up."

Brits, Frost thought. The accents were nearly unmistakable.

"Cut them loose, prepare to move. Carry them if you have to." The man in the middle of the room turned round, peering at the ground, kicking debris away here and there until…

"Ah, got him." He slung his rifle, reached down with both hands, grabbed at something and lifted. "Mr. Fischer, I presume?"

Frost felt hands working on his wrists and ankles. "Hold still, mate. These things are quite sharp."

"The girl," Frost croaked.

"We have her. Settle down, sir."

Frost felt the cold steel of a pair of snips press into his left wrist and dig for a grip on the wire. He grunted and ground his teeth together.

"Apologies, mate," the man said. "I'll try to make this quick."

The snips caught the cable, pressed, and Frost felt the pressure on his wrist release. The man repeated the process three times and pulled Frost upright. "Think you can walk?"

Frost worked up to a standing position with the man's help. He turned around, wobbled. Had to be steadied by the man in the mask. "Ewa…"

"Got her, mate. She's over there." The man helped Frost along.

Frost took a few limping steps, ignoring the pain in his wounded ankles, and reached Ewa as she was being pulled to her feet. He grabbed for her, wrapped his arms around her shoulders. She buried her face in his chest.

"One minute, sir," barked the man by the door.

Frost turned to look at him, saw the man in the middle of the room holding Fischer at gunpoint. Heard Fischer whimpering.

"No. You can't do this. It's a mistake. This is a mistake…"

"No mistake, mate." The man raised his gun. "Resh doesn't make mistakes."

Frost used his shoulders to block Ewa's view but did not turn his own head. The flash from the weapon seared his eyes, but the noise was almost non-existent. Just the pop of the cartridges, the metallic clack of the bolt cycling three times, and the wet slap of bullets tearing into Fischer's head.

Ewa jumped but made no sound. Fischer's body crumpled into a pile on the floor. The man in the middle of the room turned to the door. "Mr. Frost?"

"Yes?"

"We need you and Miss Fischer to follow us. Can you do that?"

"Who are you?"

"Time for that later. For right now, we are the people getting you out of this hell hole."

Frost looked down at Ewa, felt her arms holding tight to him, saw her upturned face. Saw the blood and the rough bandage one of the Brits had applied to her wound. Felt the urge to walk over and kick Fischer's corpse. "Can you walk?" he asked her gently. She nodded.

"Alright," Frost said to the Brits. "After you."

The man in charge stepped through the door and out into the night. The man who had sat by the door followed him, weapon up and tracing back and forth in the darkness. Frost and Ewa followed.

They walked quickly and quietly, circling the building they had just left and tucking themselves into the shadows behind it. Frost could feel the pain from his ankles arcing up his legs as they moved, with the four gunmen, from cover to cover.

It seemed absurd to Frost that there was no response. That there were not hundreds of soldiers racing to the scene of the explosion. But there was no one.

There was just the night, the sounds of crickets, and rows of what appeared to be empty huts. In the far distance, he could hear the low, growling sound of trucks rolling across uneven ground, but there were no troops and no emergency sirens.

They made their way quickly and quietly to a fence. Maybe three or four hundred yards from where they had started, according to Frost's estimate. Ewa stumbled and fell twice on the way and Frost caught her each time. She was crying silently. He could see that in the clear, silvery light of the moon. Tears were streaming down her face. She was unsteady. Wounded. Beaten. But she was moving. She kept putting one foot in front of the other.

They reached a fence and Frost saw that a section of the cross-hatched wire had been removed.

"Okay," said the man in charge. "Through here and another two hundred yards to a trail. We've got a staff car hidden there. And spare Nazi uniforms for everyone. Identification papers and orders, too. Anyone stops us and we'll pass ourselves off as a unit out from the main inspectorate. Any questions?"

Frost had questions, but he kept them to himself for the time being. He pulled himself through the hole in the wire and helped Ewa through. The four gunmen came next, and the group resumed their original formation. Two gunmen in front, Frost and Ewa in the middle, and two gunmen in the rear.

The two-hundred-yard trek took another ten minutes. They moved slowly and carefully and made as little noise as possible as they walked through the thick forest. When they came across the trail and the staff car, the gunmen went to work.

"Everything's in the boot," said the man in charge. "Mr. Frost, we have your exact sizes. Apologies to you, Miss Fischer, but we had to guess on yours. Resh wasn't sure, and there was no time to check."

One of the men opened the car and began handing out gear. The men changed quickly near the car. Frost helped Ewa to a stand of bushes nearby and then returned to the men, and she ducked behind it to dress.

"She's going to be okay, sir," said the man in charge. "Seems to be a tough trooper."

"She hasn't said a word," Frost noted. "Not a word."

"Give her time, sir," the man advised. "Aside from whatever her brother did to her, he was her brother, and we just shot the bastard right in front of her."

"And who are you?"

"Can't say."

"Can't say, or won't?" Frost asked, pulling on a set of freshly polished boots.

The man shrugged and pulled a necktie on.

"Who sent you? Who's this Resh character?"

"I'm afraid I can't tell you, sir," said the man. "Not part of my brief, you see."

Frost glared at the man. The man stared back, pulling his tie tight against the collar.

"Best I can tell you is that we had orders to break you out of that place. Didn't start that way. Original orders had us killing you and Fischer and the girl. But something changed. A chap named Thornhill got involved, passed your name on to Resh, and Resh told us to keep you alive. You and the girl. We get you two out. Kill the spare. And take you to the nearest border. A place called Siekierki, to be precise. A little town just across the Oder." The man checked his watch. "And to do that last part, we need to hurry."

"Worried about people chasing us down?"

The man looked around at his comrades. Ewa came out from behind the bushes, her hands busy pressing the wrinkles out of her uniform.

"No, he's not," she said. Her voice was light and brittle, but confident. "It's because it is nearly four in the morning on September first."

Frost looked from Ewa to the Brits, and back. "I'm sorry. I don't understand…"

Ewa moved closer to the group, then walked up to Frost and adjusted his necktie, tucking the loose end into his shirt between the third and fourth buttons. "In two hours, the German Army will drive into Poland."

She made the statement plainly and matter-of-factly, as if she'd just stated her plans for dinner or a coming holiday in Italy.

"Excuse me?" Frost thought to ask how she knew, but didn't. He could guess. Elias.

"She is quite right, sir," said the man in charge, now in the uniform of a Wehrmacht colonel, like everyone else. "Which leaves us precious little time to get you to those bridges."

Everyone began climbing into the staff car. Frost helped Ewa into the backseat, then piled in with her and one of the gunmen. The man in charge started the car. The engine purred. He shifted into gear and moved the car along the trail and out onto the main road. The man beside him turned and answered a question Frost had not voiced.

"You see, sir," he said, "if we're late, your paths into Poland get fairly bleak. The minute that first Panzer rolls onto the bridge, the Poles are likely to blow the damned thing. Even if it is in Nazi territory right now."

Frost grimaced. *And if I don't make it across before then, Ewa and I will have to swim the Oder in the middle of a running battle.*

Lovely.

The drive took the group north, away from Oranienburg, before turning east toward Liebenwalde, Falkenberg, and, eventually, the German–Polish border. The ride was mainly conducted in silence, with the occasional question put forth by Frost. Some were answered. Most were not. The gunmen refused to give their names but did admit their British origins. They refused to talk about their orders. Refused to talk about Resh. And the only time Frost brought up VEIL, the driver flinched visibly.

He was, however, able to gather information about the facility they had escaped.

"Hell on earth, mate, if you fall into the wrong category," said the driver.

"Wrong category?"

"Undesirables," said the man next to Ewa. "Folks the Nazis don't want running around in the open." He paused, looked at Frost, and continued. "Criminals, mostly. For now. Some others. Gays. Gypsies. Folks with disabilities. Jews."

"They just lock people up?" The question sounded terribly naïve, but Frost said it anyway.

To his surprise, Ewa laughed.

"What?"

"The lucky ones get locked up. In regular prisons. But places like that…" She shook her head. "They are labor camps. Work camps." She paused, seemed to struggle with something, then turned and looked at Frost. "People like my brother run their prisoners into the ground. Starve them. Abuse them. Work them to death on whatever the Nazi war machine needs. And, when it becomes necessary, when they need to make room for newer inmates or, frankly, whenever the mood strikes them, they march these people into special rooms at the camp and exterminate them."

"The lady is right, sir," said the driver. "We used to call that genocide. Hitler and his goons are rounding up people whom they deem as threats to racial purity and eradicating them. No joke. We've seen three of the places during our travels. There's one with this iron gate out front and a little motto welded into it. *Arbeit macht frei*, it says."

"Work sets you free," Frost translated.

The driver nodded, steered around a turn. "Couple of lies for the price of one, sir." He edged the car around an elderly man on a bicycle and drove on. The man on the bicycle yelled as they drove by, a faint "Heil Hitler" following them down the road.

Frost let him drive in silence, kept his arm around Ewa. Looked at her.

"Are you okay?"

Ewa turned her face into his shoulder, did not lift her eyes to meet his. "Is it true?"

"Is what true?" he asked, suspecting that he knew damned good and well what she meant.

"You are a spy?"

Jesus, he thought. How to answer that?

He got some unexpected assistance from the driver.

"No, Miss Fischer," he said, a thin slice of amusement in his voice. "Mr. Frost here is most definitely not a spy. Not a trained one, anyway. He's just some dumb bootneck they sent to pick up a folder. Haven't even paid him properly."

The man in the right front seat turned and grinned at Frost. Frost smiled back.

"Is that true?" Ewa asked.

Frost almost laughed as the car bounced and roared along. He started to speak, but the man next to Frost cut him off. "Of course, it's true, mum. Only a bloody bootneck could get himself into such a mess."

Frost looked down at Ewa. She was looking at him. She was smiling. "So, if you aren't really a spy…"

"What's next?" he asked. "Hell if I know. I'd like to get home safely. Probably farm or find a job somewhere. Something honest and a hell of a lot less dangerous."

"And did you really get kicked out of the American Marines?"

The driver answered for him again. "That he did, mum." A pause as he turned south. "And yes, he did punch his commanding officer in the nose. Not very dignified, but…"

Frost looked curiously at the driver, his head cocked to the side. A question flashed through his mind and he asked it.

"How is it you know so much about me?"

He saw the three gunmen in the front seat exchange looks with each other. He waited, not really expecting an answer. He did, eventually, get one. And when he heard it, he was not surprised. Just confused.

"Resh."

He wanted to ask about Resh. Who or what he was. Was Resh even a person? It didn't much sound like a name to him. He opened his mouth to speak, to start firing away with a fresh battery of questions, but a small, soft, warm hand reached up and touched his jaw. Turned his face down.

He could see Ewa in the light of the moon. Could see her clearly. Could see her swollen jaw and split lip and dirty, bandaged face. Could see her wincing with every jolt of the car. Could see the tracks her tears had made down her cheeks.

She lifted her face to his and kissed him, then pulled away from him, smiling through the pain.

"Shut up, Frost."

Frost shut up. He held her shoulders tight, felt her warmth beside him as the driver navigated his way through the forest roads of eastern Germany.

15 | Crossing

The driver pulled the car off the road, directing it carefully onto a spur and then off into a collection of trees two hundred yards from the dirt highway they'd just left. They'd spent the past hour moving south, using backroads mostly, to pick and wind their way closer to the bridges at Siekierki. They'd moved slowly through the area, with the headlamps doused and with little or no conversation as they moved from checkpoint to checkpoint, none of which had given them much more than a cursory look and wild, enthusiastic salutes as they passed.

The driver stopped the car and everyone exited, stretching and yawning. Frost's ankles and wrists were swollen and painful, and he found that each step required care. He was busying himself checking on Ewa—kneeling in front of her and checking on the shallow cuts the wire restraints had made on her ankles—when one of the gunmen tapped him on the shoulder. Frost stood and turned. The man was holding a pile of clothes.

"New uniforms, sir," he said. "Polish Cavalry. Should match what the blokes in Poznan are wearing. Got papers too. For the both of you." He looked at Ewa rather sheepishly.

"Sorry, mum, if that seems improper. Resh told us to assume that you would be accompanying Mr. Frost here into Poland."

Frost looked at Ewa. He cocked an eyebrow. "What do you think?"

Ewa did not hesitate. She reached for a uniform and turned to find a place to change.

"Not yet, mum."

Ewa turned back. "Pardon?"

"I wouldn't change yet," the driver answered. "The bridge crossing is technically in German territory. And so is the land beyond. For maybe forty kilometers or so. You change into those now, and the Germans will most certainly shoot you as you work your way east."

Frost turned to the driver. "I take it you aren't coming with us?"

The driver shook his head, began pulling several heavy packs from the staff car's boot. "No, sir. Resh has more work for us to do here."

"I see," Frost said, taking the spare uniform and holding it up. "And I gather that you're still not going to tell me who this Resh person is? Or anything about this organization you work for?"

"No, sir. Again, not part of my brief," the driver said, hefting the last of the packs out onto the ground.

"It occurs to me that this Resh seems to be playing both sides," Frost offered, hoping for a nibble.

"Don't know what you mean, sir," said the driver.

"He was clearly supporting Elias Fischer. A Nazi. Right up until the moment you shot Elias in the head. But you also take orders from this Resh and you're Brits. Presumably on the other side when this war kicks off. He's ordered you to help me escape. And I'm an American." A thought occurred to Frost, something he'd not realized before. Or, rather, something that his mind had caught and which he'd not yet analyzed. "And there's one other thing. Fischer was interrogating me. Threatening me. Threatening her. And then, in a flash, everything changed. The entire course of the conversation. Like his brain just snapped. Locked onto something. Fischer seemed awfully concerned that I knew Thornhill. That I'd met him in Shanghai. That he and I were somehow in league with each other. That I knew Resh. Or Resh knew me."

"I can't speak to that, sir," said the driver. "I was just told to find you, eliminate Mr. Fischer, and get you and the lady here to the river crossing."

Frost stared, told himself that he'd get nothing more from the man, shook his head. Later, he thought. There will be time for this later.

The driver tugged at his sleeve, revealed his watch. "It's nearly dawn, sir. You and the lady should get going."

Frost was still watching the man, saw the sleeve being tugged down into place. In the faint light, he thought he caught an imprint of something on the underside of the man's wrist. A capital 'V' with a small circle between the upright portions of the letter. It was curious, he thought. An odd tattoo, and an odd place for one. But he ignored it. He'd known men with tattoos before, had seen some fairly strange ones. And in some fairly unique places.

And, at the moment, he had more important things to worry about. He walked to where Ewa was standing, close to the edge of the tree line.

"Are you sure about this?"

She turned to him, lifted her face. He saw that she'd been crying again. She wiped at the tears and winced. It must have hurt like hell, Frost thought.

"You want to go with me?"

She nodded again. "Yes. There's nothing left for me here. And even if there was…" She let her voice trail off into the lightening sky.

Yeah, Frost thought. And even if there was…

"You should get going," the driver called over quietly.

Frost turned to look at him, saw that the four men had donned their packs, were busy cinching the straps. Saw one collect his rifle.

"There are some rations in the car," the driver said. "Get across the bridge and head east as best you can. Stay off the main roads and keep north of the line from Frankfurt to Poznan. Our sources tell us that the main thrust will come from the south, with Guderian's Panzers—"

"Was ist das? Wer bist du?" a voice behind Frost interrupted the driver. *What is this? Who are you?*

Frost turned, saw two men in Wehrmacht uniforms emerging from the thickest part of the woods. As he watched, four more men emerged. Six in total. Three with short, black machine guns. Three with older, bolt-action rifles. They looked surprised to see anyone here in this part of the forest. They looked even more surprised to see a collection of people dressed as colonels. The first two started to come to attention, but stopped, their eyes drifting to Ewa. There was a curiosity on their faces that Frost immediately did not trust. Something he'd not seen in the faces of the two dozen checkpoint guards.

There was a wildness to their eyes that he could see even in the poor light. And slight tremors in their hands. Two of the men seemed to have nervous tics, one a twitch on his face and the other, a need to constantly be moving, shifting from foot to foot.

Damnit. Be cool, he thought. Let's everybody be cool.

"My apologies, Colonel," one of the men, the one with sergeant's stripes, said. "We were not told to expect anyone in this sector."

His eyes were moving, Frost saw. From the driver, to some of the other gunmen, to himself, and then back to Ewa. Always back to Ewa. To her face.

The driver stepped forward, smiling. "Nothing to apologize for, Sergeant…?"

The man snapped to, his heels clicking together and his right arm rising. "Meyer, Colonel. Sergeant Hermann Meyer of the Frontier Guards."

The driver returned the salute, still smiling. "As you were, Sergeant Meyer. As you were." He looked around, then made a show of checking his watch. "You and your men are early, yes?"

The sergeant did not answer. His eyes kept moving back and forth. He looked at the staff car, at the collection of colonels, at the three submachine guns propped against the car. And back to Ewa. To her face. It was just light enough, Frost thought, for the sergeant to see her injuries. Even from fifteen feet away.

"Geht es ihr gut?" the sergeant asked. *Is she okay?*

The driver turned, looked back at Ewa, and spat in the dirt. He growled. "She is now. Polish soldiers. We stopped for a stretch after inspecting the checkpoints north of here and she stumbled upon a small band of Poles heading east. They beat her, as you can see, but we scared them off." He moved closer to the sergeant. "Bastards. All of them. Criminal sonsofbitches. Just as the Führer says."

Frost watched the sergeant closely, kept watching his eyes, watched how they shifted from person to person. It was as if he knew instinctively that something in front of him did not fit, but could not say, precisely, what might be wrong.

"Excuse me, Colonel," the sergeant said. "It may seem improper, but could I see your papers?"

The driver slapped the man on the shoulder, laughed. "Not improper, Sergeant. Not improper at all. Can't be too careful on a day like this. Not with the fate of the Fatherland hanging in the balance." He turned to his men, to Frost, and to Ewa. "Please, everyone, your papers. All of you. Let him see them."

Frost saw the driver and two of the other gunmen—the men who'd been in the front seat of the staff car—dig in their pockets and produce their forged identification papers. The third gunman, he saw to his horror, had, at some point, unslung his rifle and had it in front of him at the low ready. One of the soldiers—a private—also noticed this and moved forward, further into the clearing, pointing at the gunman, his voice agitated.

"Was machst du?" he said, his own weapon coming unslung. *What are you doing?*

The private's eyes traced the scene wildly. There was a visible tremor in his hands as the rifle's barrel kept coming up. He paused, the rifle pointed at the gunman's knees, his eyes now locked on the pile of Polish clothes beside Ewa.

"Sergeant!" he shrieked. "Sie haben Polnische uniformen!"

The sergeant turned to see what his private was shrieking about and Frost saw his eyes go wide. His left shoulder dropped, the bolt-action rifle falling into his hands as he tried to step back, away from the colonel.

The driver moved like lightning. He swatted the moving rifle down with his left hand and stepped behind the sergeant. His right arm clamped around the sergeant's neck and a knife appearing, its razor-sharp edge glinting and pressing against the sergeant's throat.

"Drop the weapons!" he ordered the collection of privates, in German. "Drop them now."

The sergeant's men held firm. Three more had managed to unsling their weapons and raise them to hip level.

The driver backed up two steps, dragging the shorter sergeant nearer to the car.

"Drop the guns!" he ordered again. Another step back. And one to the side, placing the sergeant directly between the nervous soldiers and Frost.

The sergeant's men edged closer, all five of them now with their weapons up.

"In the car, Herr Frost," the driver muttered, still moving backward. "Get in the car and go. Now!"

Frost grabbed Ewa's hand and began moving toward the car, careful to keep the driver and his captive between them and the soldiers.

"Stoppen. Hören Sie jetzt auf, sonst schießen wir," the private yelled. *Stop or we'll shoot!*

"Get moving, Herr Frost," ordered the driver. "Get in the car and get moving."

"Ridge?" Ewa said. She was nearly frozen in place and Frost found that moving her was difficult.

"In the car," Frost said. "We have to go."

"What about…"

The private and one of the other soldiers were barking orders in rapid-fire German, their voices strained and wavering.

"Forget about us," the driver growled. "Get in the fucking car and go!"

Frost and Ewa were within arm's reach of the car's rear when the first shot rang out. The bullet punched a neat hole in the driver's side door, not two feet from Ewa's knees.

The fourth gunman, the only one with his weapon, dropped to his knees and opened fire, spraying the soldiers for all he was worth, his silenced submachine gun spitting and clacking, the noise ricocheting off the surrounding trees.

The three privates on the left went down. Two with wounds to the chest and gut, the third taking one round to the shoulder and one to his throat. The two soldiers blocked by the driver and his hostage dove for cover, hitting the ground and rolling.

"Fucking hell," yelled the driver, switching back to English. He dropped to one knee, dragging the sergeant to the ground with him. His hands yanked in opposite directions as he dropped, slicing a neat, deep line across the sergeant's neck.

He shoved the sergeant forward and rolled to the side, toward where the three remaining rifles were stacked, reaching and groping for one as he got back on his feet and bounded across the ground.

Frost shoved Ewa forward, screaming. "In the car!"

She moved, diving in through the open door and scrambling to make room for Frost to follow. Frost threw himself into the car, knocking Ewa flat across the seat and reaching for the ignition. Bullets spanged against the hard metal body of the car as the two remaining German soldiers stopped rolling and opened fire from prone positions thirty feet away.

Frost heard an audible grunt as he worked to start the engine and heard something heavy collide with the car's rear passenger door. He cranked the ignition, heard the car rumble and cough and stop. Frost swore. He cranked the ignition again.

A bullet tore through the door panel and slammed into his left leg. Frost's hand came off the ignition and grabbed at his thigh. His upper leg was on fire, blood streaming out of the wound.

"Shit!"

Ewa screamed and leaned over him, shoving his head down and reaching for the ignition. She grabbed it and turned. The engine coughed. It sputtered. Bullets continued slamming into the metal body. Bullets shattered the driver's side windows, flinging glass over both of them. She turned the ignition again.

The engine coughed.

The engine rumbled.

The engine caught.

Frost heard the engine start. He heard Ewa screaming. He lifted himself up slightly, threw the car into gear, and stomped on the gas.

For an eternity, it seemed like the car would not move. Amid the snap of flying bullets and the screaming of fighting and wounded men, Frost could hear the tires grinding away in the gravel and dirt. He screamed at the car. Pleaded with it. Cursed it.

"Come on, you piece of shit!"

The tires gained purchase and the car shot forward, a hail of bullets following and passing it. The rear window exploded. Bullets slammed into the boot. Into the seats. Frost grabbed Ewa with his right hand and shoved her down onto the floorboards while he steered with his left.

A bullet crashed into his right shoulder, threw him forward into the steering column. The car swerved toward the stand of trees just near the edge of the road. Frost ground his teeth against the pain, felt his shoulder burning and his arm going numb. Felt the searing heat there. And the fire in his left thigh. He yanked hard on the wheel with his left hand, pointed the nose of the rampaging car at a gap in the trees.

"Hold on," he barked.

The car slammed into the bank and caromed over the edge and onto the main road. Frost yanked down hard on the wheel again, steering the car onto the road as best he could. He caught the oversteer just before the car plummeted off into the ditch and slowly worked to bring it under control.

He could still hear gunshots behind him, but there were no sounds of impacts. He gritted his teeth against the pain, tried to use his right arm to shift gears. The wrenching pain there stopped him, brought tears to his eyes. Beside him, Ewa started to climb off the floorboards.

"Not yet," he growled.

She ignored him, pulled herself onto the seat, her eyes wide in horror. "Ridge…"

"I'm fine…" he croaked. His body was starting to shake. He felt a coolness inside that he thought could not be good.

Blood loss, his brain said.

"You're not fine," Ewa argued. She leaned over the back seat. "There has to be something here…"

Frost pulled her back to the front seat with his damaged right arm, the effort launching bolts of pain down his arm and across his back.

The car swerved and he barely caught it. He ground his teeth against each other, hard, fearing that they might crack or crumble or break with the pressure. His vision blurred, a slight softening around the edges that narrowed his line of sight. He fought desperately to keep the car centered on the road. Fought to focus, to clear the cobwebs his injuries were inflicting. On the road. On the sun that was just beginning to creep over the horizon.

He whispered a silent prayer of thanks that he'd somehow turned east amid the chaos of the gunfight. A fresh wave of pain rushed over him. Beside him, he heard a slight ripping noise. He turned, saw that Ewa had removed her uniform jacket, was tearing at the seams. Watched as she yanked the lining loose. He felt the car haul to the right. Heard the crunching of tires screaming through gravel.

Ewa swore. "Watch the road!"

Frost snapped his head forward, pulled left on the wheel, guided the car back onto the road.

His vision blurred again. Heavier this time. He leaned right, felt that he could not hold himself upright. The car veered with him.

Ewa shoved him upright, pressing against his damaged shoulder and sending fiery tendrils of pain tearing through his body.

"Fuck!" His vision cleared. He yanked the wheel left.

"Pull to the side!" Ewa order. "Before you get us both killed."

"Not far enough…" he muttered weakly.

She reached in front of him, grabbed the right side of the wheel, started turning it. "Foot off the gas, Frost."

"No…" he argued. "Not yet…"

"Now, Frost," she repeated. "Foot off the damned gas!"

Frost felt his head lolling to the side, felt his arm and side and leg going numb again. Felt the cold creeping over his body. His vision ebbed away, replaced by a solid fog that was completely impenetrable. He eased his foot off the gas, felt the car rolling onto the shoulder as he slumped toward his left. Heard the slow crunching of gravel under the tires. He tried to shake his head clear, to lift it before it made contact with the door frame and the shattered glass there, but it was too heavy. Too hard.

Much easier to just close my eyes, he thought. Just need a nap. A quick one.

"Ridge!" a woman's voice was yelling. "Wake up, Ridge!"

There was a faint stab of pain on the side of his face as it came to rest on the top of the door panel. His eyes drifted closed.

It's quiet here, he thought. Quiet in the dark. Except…

There's a voice. Whose?

"Stay awake, Ridge. Stay with me."

No, he thought. Need to rest. Must rest.

The voice was drifting on him. He could barely hear it. "Ridge! Please!"

Frost breathed in. He exhaled. The coldness was going away. It was warm now. Warm and quiet and calm.

Epilogue | In

Frost felt his body moving, knew that it was not him causing the motion. He was on his back, could feel every jostle and bump. In his shoulder and arm. In his leg. Could feel tight pressure in both places. Something close and binding and restricting. He forced his eyes open. Blinked against the bright light of day, found himself looking up at the sky. At the sun and small wisps of clouds. And smoke. Thick, black smoke. Roiling on the wind.

There were voices around him. Loud and angry. Yelling. Barking. Foreign. Screaming in a language he could not understand.

There were faces above him now. Young faces. Men's faces. Blackened.

Except…

That one…

One soft face. Soft and bruised and pale. Blonde.

He felt a hand touching his forehead. Felt the warmth there. Smiled at it. Closed his eyes. Felt a stab of pain in his left arm, his good one. Wondered at it. Felt everything start to wash away. Saw the sky and faces above him blur and fade.

He felt himself falling and he allowed it, letting the world go black again.

———

Frost felt the hand long before he opened his eyes. It was small and warm and holding his own hand lightly, as if applying pressure might cause some injury. He forced his eyes open and slammed them shut again against the harsh lights above him.

"Ridge?" A voice drifted to him. Faint and light and…

Familiar?

"Ridge?"

He tried to lock onto the voice, tried to pinpoint it. Tried to move his head to look for it, dreaded opening his eyes, but he forced them wide. He turned left first, then tried to look right. White-hot, searing pain stopped him in his tracks. His teeth ground. A grunt of pain squeezed its way out of his mouth.

"Don't move, darling," said the voice. "Relax…"

The pain blazed through him. His whole body tensed. His eyes slammed shut. Nausea washed over him. There was a scrabbling of voices around him, drowning out the one he'd heard first.

He did not feel the pinprick in his arm.

He did feel his muscles relent, felt his body dissolve back into nothingness.

Back into the black.

———

Frost's eyes snapped open, blinked against the light as his pupils adjusted for the shift from black to white. He focused on the ceiling, decided it was tiled and oddly geometric. Perfect squares. Each one dotted with little black holes. Only occasionally interrupted by a hanging light. He wondered where he was.

He felt heavy, as if the entire world was resting atop his lanky frame. His mouth was dry and he tried to lick his lips, succeeded only in getting his tongue stuck to his lower lip, a condition that required a disproportionate amount of effort to correct. He tried to lift his head, but found that he lacked the strength.

"Hello," he croaked, the words sounding foreign to his own ears. "Anyone there?"

"Was wondering when you'd wake up," a voice said.

A face appeared over his bed and Frost had to blink several times before his eyes would refocus on the closer image.

"Henry?"

"It's me, kid." The face smiled. "How you feeling?"

Frost tried to swallow, felt that his tongue was now glued to the roof of his mouth. "Water?"

The face above him retreated for a moment, then returned. A cup was placed to his lips and tilted and Frost drank greedily, swallowing huge gulps down as fast as was possible.

"Easy, kid. Doc says you aren't supposed to just guzzle it down like that." The face left again, returned without the cup. "So, how are you?"

"Where am I?" Frost forced the words out with great effort. His mouth was still dry.

"England," said Henry. "Got you out on a plane. Barely. Up northeast through Poland. On to Denmark. And so forth. Took nearly a week. You were out most of the time. Damned Kraut air force nearly put paid to both our accounts. Three times. But we made it. Lost five escorts along the way." Henry paused, took a deep breath. "You did a hell of a job, though."

"I did what?" Frost asked, confused.

"Came through, kid. Big time. We've already sent both dossiers on home."

"Dossiers? What…"

"The one we sent you for wasn't very big, and frankly, I can't make heads or tails of it. Maybe Einstein or Szilard can. I assume they can. But the other dossier. Holy Christ on a crutch, son."

Frost tried to push himself upright, failed miserably.

"Hold on," Henry said. "There's a lever here somewhere. The nurse showed me." He fumbled with the side of the bed for a moment. Frost heard a click and a squeal and felt the top half of the bed lifting him into a sitting position.

Henry looked at the bed, smiled. "That'll do it, I guess."

"What dossiers, Henry? I didn't get any dossiers."

Henry's brow wrinkled. He shrugged. "You came with two folders. One with the atomic crap in it. And the other one…" He shook his head. "Fucking hell, son. Horrifying stuff. Camps where they're exterminating people they don't like. Working folks to death. Gassing them. File listed seven known places and five suspected places, including the place that this Fischer guy took you to tune you up. Statements. Recon photographs. Sick shit, kid. Real sick shit. Shit that's gonna make Roosevelt's head explode."

"But I didn't get the files," Frost said, his voice cracking and strained.

Henry shrugged again. "I'm not looking a gift horse in the mouth, kid. You went. You came back. With the files we sent you for and a little extra. That's good enough for me. A win's a win, kid."

Frost tried to ask a question, but Henry just kept going.

"When you get out of this place, and you get back home, I've got a permanent job for you."

"Doing this?" Frost croaked again. He swore at himself. Tried to clear his throat. Partially succeeded. "Thanks, but no thanks."

"I figured as much," Henry said. He pointed at Frost's shoulder. "You didn't exactly sign on for this part." He turned, moved to a nearby table, came back holding an envelope. "Had this taken care of while you were out of it." He laid the envelope on Frost's lap.

"What's this?"

"Called up that General Whitehead of yours…"

Frost tensed at the name. Henry chuckled.

"Relax, kid. He and I had a little sit-down. I gave him some information. He and I came to an understanding."

Frost eyed the envelope warily.

Henry pointed at it. "That right there is your honorable discharge from the United States Marine Corps."

Frost tried to speak, found that his mouth still felt like cotton. He smacked his lips together, took a measure of his body. There was a throbbing ache in his left thigh and a marginally larger burning sensation in his right shoulder. The left side of his face burned and he could feel the bulk of padded bandage and tape there.

I was shot, he reminded himself. Twice. But…

"What the hell happened to my face?" he croaked. He cleared his throat again. Coughed as gently as he could. "I mean, I remember the leg and my arm…"

"I am told that you passed out and dropped your face right on the broken window glass of the car you took over the Polish border." Henry said. "Lady said you were just driving all over the damned road and…"

Lady?

Shit.

Ewa.

"Where is she, Henry?"

"Who, the Fischer woman?"

"Yes. Ewa," Frost said. He felt his face flush, could feel his pulse racing away. In his neck. In his chest. In his ears. "Her name is Ewa. Where is she?"

Henry swallowed. Hard. His eyes shifted.

Frost tried to reach out with his left hand to grab Henry, but the big man was just out of range. "What, Henry? Where the hell is she?"

"The Poles have her," Henry said softly. "They've got her in prison in Gdansk. That woman drove nearly forty klicks with one hand while the other held bandages in place. All through Nazi territory and in a staff car full of secret docs and Polish uniforms and bullet holes."

Frost felt his heart sink, felt rage building. "Prison?"

"Sorry, kid," Henry said. "She's a German citizen and she crossed into Poland wearing a Nazi uniform. Hell, son.

She's lucky as hell they didn't shoot her on sight." He paused. "Lucky I was there or they'd have shot you both. It was all I could do to get you freed. The Poles got fucking slaughtered last week and they are in a foul mood."

"Is she still alive?" Frost's voice barely rose above a whisper.

"She was when we left."

Frost stayed quiet. Felt the pulsing in his head. Felt the anger swelling inside him. He glared at the envelope in his lap. Turned his head and glared at Henry.

"What?"

"I'm in."

"In?"

"I'll take the job."

Henry backed away warily. Cocked his head to one side. "Listen, kid. I know what you're—"

"I'm in, Henry."

"You can't go into Poland after her, son," Henry protested. "You—"

"I can," Frost growled. "I can and I will. Call it a condition of employment."

ABOUT THE AUTHOR

Matt Hardman is a retired U.S. Navy Chief Petty Officer who currently works as a marine engineering consultant to the Navy's DDG 51 Shipbuilding Program Office. While on active duty, he served onboard a submarine, two aircraft carriers, two amphibious transports, one submarine tender, and one destroyer. During his final tour of duty, he served as the Engineering Department Chief, or "Top Snipe," for the USS James E. Williams (DDG 95). He holds a bachelor's in Intelligence Studies and Counterintelligence from American Military University and a Master's in Writing from Johns Hopkins University.

Matt Hardman is also a husband and father of six children and currently resides in Calvert County, Maryland.

DOUBLE‡DAGGER
— www.doubledagger.ca —

Double Dagger Books is Canada's only military-focused publisher. Conflict and warfare have shaped human history since before we began to record it. The earliest stories that we know of, passed on as oral tradition, speak of war, and more importantly, the essential elements of the human condition that are revealed under its pressure.

We are dedicated to publishing material that, while rooted in conflict, transcend the idea of "war" as merely a genre. Fiction, non-fiction, and stuff that defies categorization, we want to read it all.

Because if you want peace, study war.

www.ingramcontent.com/pod-product-compliance
Lightning Source LLC
Chambersburg PA
CBHW040905010826
48978CB00013BB/1157